A MEDIA DEBUT FOR MURDER

It was the worst possible time for murder. Radio Broadwich had come to do a documentary on Twytching's local charm. Mrs. Withens, self-appointed arbiter of community affairs, was determined to see the town put its best foot forward —a Herculean task, what with Reverend Tamville-Bence practising exorcisms and holding séances . . . with Mrs. Buller's voluptuous daughter clearly in the family way without her husband's help . . . with tall, elegant Alison Mailer using all her wiles to get interviewed on the air . . . and with handsome schoolmaster Jack Edgar making eyes at flamboyant Harold Thring, Radio Broadwich's assistant producer.

But when violent death tarnished little Twytching's snug image, it was up to Police Inspector George Parrish to let the skeletons out of the cottage closets and sweep the scandals out from under the beds . . . and to use what old Amos Chipweather saw to catch a killer.

And don't forget the other excellent Scene Of The Crime®
and Murder Ink.® Mysteries.

A Scene Of The Crime® Mystery

A LITTLE LOCAL MURDER

Robert Barnard

A DELL BOOK

Published by
Dell Publishing Co., Inc.
1 Dag Hammarskjold Plaza
New York, New York 10017

Dell ® TM 681510, Dell Publishing Co., Inc.

ISBN: 0-440-14882-0

Reprinted by arrangement with Charles Scribner's Sons.

Printed in the United States of America
First Dell printing—March 1984
D D

CONTENTS

CHAPTER I

HOW THE GOOD NEWS
WAS BROUGHT

The letter arrived on the front doormat of Glencoe, the residence of the Chairman of the Twytching District Council, on Wednesday morning, but (the Chairman being busy in the kitchen frying bacon and mushrooms, poaching eggs and toasting toast) it was some time before he came to hear of its contents. Instead the Chairman's lady wife, who liked people to call her the Mayoress, consented to bend her substantial frame in the course of her progress from the bedroom to the breakfast room and collect it with all the rest of the official mail. Once seated she spread the letters fan-like around her breakfast plate. Then she settled her bosom comfortably on to the table and tucked genteely into her porridge.

The words 'Radio Broadwich' on the long envelope in the middle of her fan of letters caught her eye as the first spoonful of the smooth scalding liquid began its journey down her throat. Drawn from the fan, the envelope revealed further, in small print, the words 'serving East Anglia and the South East'. Deborah Withens furrowed her brow, and thoughtfully stirred a modicum of brown sugar into the porridge. Radio Broadwich. Now that was odd. Her communications with the BBC had been many and unhappy, though in fact they had not been favoured with a missive from her for many months, for the courteous rationality of their replies – 'sheer evasion' she called it – had sat heavily on her bosom. Recently she had channelled her remarks through Mrs Margaret Lightfoot of the League for the Preservation of Decent Standards in Radio and

Television, and had been highly satisfied with the amount of publicity accorded the screened indecencies she had witnessed. But this letter could be about none of her recent complaints – not about the scandalous reference to *coitus interruptus* on *Woman's Hour,* nor about the bare-breasted dancing by Ibo tribeswomen shown on Children's Television. Radio Broadwich, she felt sure, was a commercial radio station, though in point of fact she had to admit to herself that she had never actually listened to it. Tireless though she was in her efforts to combat the rising flood of indecency, still, there were limits to the amount of time one could devote to it, and the number of ears. Then again, a great deal of their output was pop music, and she knew from her contacts with other members of the Decent Standards League that the search for concealed meanings in pop songs could lead only to frustration, madness and public ridicule, none of which were fates Mrs Withens had any intention of bringing on herself.

This, then, must be some other matter, but what could it be? Mrs Withens blew a lady-like breath in the direction of the porridge, and was about to open the letter when she saw that it was in fact addressed not to herself but to her husband. Her husband! Doubly inquisitive, she inserted a pudgy finger into the opening at the top, and tore it open.

Two good mouthfuls of porridge later, an observer would have been surprised to see a smile spreading over her face. An observer well acquainted with Mrs Withens would always be surprised to see a smile spreading over her face. It was, to be sure, a steely, determined smile, a smile portending triumphs to come, and it disappeared before she majestically drew porridge-flecked air into her majestic lungs, and bellowed: 'Ernest!'

From the kitchen there came a series of puppyish whines and a clatter of pans, and a minute or so later Ernest Withens, Chairman of the Twytching District Council, came puffing in, an apron around his ample middle, and a plate of assorted breakfast goodies in his hand. Mrs

Withens observed him arrive, raised her eyebrows by a
decimal point, and allowed a couple of seconds to elapse
in eloquent silence before she threw her eyes down to her
porridge plate and said : 'I have not as yet finished my
porridge, Ernest.'

The words were not in themselves striking, but the
pauses between them were immensely telling. Mr Withens
emitted further whimpers of apology and backed with his
plate towards the kitchen.

'Leave it, leave it,' said Mrs Withens, with an autumnal
intonation, 'you know I *detest* warmed-up food. I must
just hurry with my porridge, I suppose – at whatever cost
to my indigestion.'

And she tucked in with a will, while Mr Withens stood
to apologetic attention and waited for illumination. Finally,
with a delicate belch which she caught in her napkin, Mrs
Withens pushed her plate from her, drew towards her the
eggs, bacon and mushrooms, and examined the knife and
fork for any signs of slovenly washing up. Finally, as she
poised her knife to break the egg over the bacon and toast,
she said : 'You have been written to, Ernest, by a gentleman at Radio Broadwich.'

'Really, Deborah?' said Mr Withens. He did not com-
plain that she had opened his mail. That protest had been
made on 7th February 1947, after four months of marriage.
It had not been renewed. Mr Withens waited.

'They are intending, Ernest, to visit Twytching in the
very near future.'

'Really, Deborah?' said Mr Withens again. 'I didn't
know you had made any complaints about their programmes.' Taking advantage of a pause necessitated by
the thorough mastication of a large, succulent mushroom,
he added ingratiatingly : 'They must have been very impressed by your letter if they think of paying you a visit.'

Mrs Withens sighed heavily. 'If you would listen to me,
Ernest, just once in a while, you would have heard me
say that the letter was addressed to you. The visit, there-

fore, has nothing whatsoever to do with my monitoring work for the Decent Standards League.'

'No, of course not, Deborah,' said Ernest Withens.

'Radio Broadwich,' said Mrs Withens, slowly and impressively, 'is intending to make a documentary programme about Twytching. To be sent to America, and broadcast over a Wisconsin radio station. I presume you understand why?'

Light indeed seemed to have dawned.

'Our twin town,' said Ernest Withens. 'Twytching, Wis.'

'Precisely,' said his wife. 'One feels one's labours have not been in vain.'

The royal 'one' so modestly used by Deborah Withens should not be allowed to conceal the fact that her pat was on her own back, and was thoroughly justified. As soon as her husband attained his present exalted office, she had ordered him to make contact with his opposite number in Twytching, Wis. (a town of some forty thousand American souls), and the twinning had been arranged in no time. Before long, it was confidently expected, little knots of descendants of the founding fathers of Twytching, Wis., would be trickling each summer back to Twytching, England, in search of their roots. Already Mrs Withens had exchanged several letters with the Mayoress (*how* she begrudged her the title!) of Twytching, Wis., a blue-rinsed virago who scented publicity and future free accommodation from the twinning. Gush and condescension alternated in the correspondence, the lady of Twytching, Wis., being particularly strong in the former quality, the lady of Twytching, England, quite unparalleled in the latter. All in all, it had been a marriage of true minds, and now, far from having impediments admitted, it was to be productive of a glorious offspring.

'Radio Broadwich,' said Mrs Withens impressively, 'has been contacted by the Wisconsin station. There has been, I gather, much publicity in the area concerning the twinning, and they propose a documentary nearly an hour long – allowing time for commercials. They suggest it might be called "*This is Twytching* – a portrait of an English village". We might perhaps change that to "country town", but that is a mere detail.'

'This must be most gratifying to you, Deborah,' said Ernest Withens in the self-congratulatory pause that followed. 'What form will the programme take?'

'Well, apparently they've done one before – for a town in Essex with a twin in Canada. I gather they will record some typical events and features of village life, then there will be a series of interviews with selected members of the community. A gentleman will be flown from the radio station to conduct the interviews. And then the producer says that some of those interviewed will be asked to choose a favourite piece of music to be played for their American cousins – "as light relief", he says. Hmm. But still, it sounds a very nice type of programme. A sort of *Down Your Way* specially for our American cousins. How they will enjoy it!'

'When have they said they will be coming, Deborah?'

'The middle of May, or just after. And Mr –' (here Mrs Withens peered at a lazy scrawl at the bottom of the letter) – 'Livermore, I think, says that they will send it out on Radio Broadwich as soon as it's completed, to give the locals a chance to hear it, before the tape is sent to America. What a thrill for the town! And what an opportunity!'

'Opportunity, Deborah?'

'Opportunity, Ernest,' repeated Mrs Withens in a thrilling voice, like Clara Butt tuning up. 'To put the town on the map. To show our friends in America what a really clean and decent and upstanding place England still can be, once you come outside those filthy, degenerate towns. We must make Twytching a symbol of all the old values which made England a great and decent place.'

'We, Deborah?'

'I, Ernest,' said Mrs Withens, for once accepting the

correction. 'I shall project an . . . image' (Mrs Withens had picked up all sorts of modish words while fighting shoulder to shoulder with Spotless Maggie) 'which will be a rebuke to the laxity and cynicism of the age.'

'That will be nice,' said the Chairman. 'Who else have they asked to be on, do you think?'

'As yet, they have asked no one to be on,' said Mrs Withens. 'I shall write your reply to them in the near future, making it clear that I myself will appear, and per- haps suggesting one or two other names, though we need not have a final list before they arrive here. I shall want to weigh up the pros and cons as far as certain members of the community are concerned.' There came into her eyes a glint of district-council power lust as this new oppor- tunity for dispensing patronage flowered in her brain. 'I think by the time the producer arrives here, I can have a short list which will be representative of all the various sides of life in Twytching.'

'I'm sure he'll be very grateful, dear,' said Mr Withens. 'What particular sides were you thinking of, though?'

'Well, there's . . . there's,' but for once Mrs Withens's fertile tongue came to a halt. It was very difficult to say what 'sides' there were to Twytching life, except gossip, sloth and beer-drinking. The villagers seemed to have few ambitions beyond those of reaching retirement age as quickly as possible, and remaining alive as long as possible after that, to spite the government. 'There's *education,*' she finally produced triumphantly. 'There's the school. And the church, of course.'

'Don't you think the vicar . . . ?'

'Well, no, not the vicar. Definitely not the vicar. But perhaps he could get a nice young curate by then. We wouldn't want the long hair and leather-jacket type, though. Perhaps one of the church-wardens. Or the sexton.'

'Old Everett certainly is a character,' said Mr Withens dubiously, 'but his *language* . . .'

'His language can be cleaned up, like everything else,' said Mrs Withens determinedly. 'You seem to be approaching this matter with a singularly faint heart. If you are not enthusiastic, I certainly am. We are going to put Twytching on the map. This, Ernest, will be the highlight of your period of office.'

'Really, Deborah?' said Mr Withens.

'Toast, Ernest,' said Mrs Withens, turning her attention back to everyday matters. 'Don't stand there dreaming all day. I have a hard morning's work in front of me.'

Mrs Leaze piloted her massive and ill-co-ordinated frame around the shelves of the Twytching village shop, keeping an eye on her customers in a manner she found much more satisfactory than what she called 'one of them two-way mirror things'. The village shop had recently been slightly redesigned and rechristened the village supermarket, and this reorganization meant that instead of Mrs Leaze getting things for her customers, she now told them where everything was that she felt they might or ought to need. This change suited Mrs Leaze, for the retailing of information was her forte, and she had a variety of different tones for the assorted items of information, ranging from a breezy cackle to a choked whisper. It was not for nothing that she was known to the village wits as 'Mrs Sleaze', and there were many who contended that one could judge the staple of village news by the length of petticoat showing under the hem of her dress: on dull days she remembered to hitch it up, but when there was a juicy item to be circulated from customer to customer it was allowed to drift down and down, like the floating pound. Today there was a good six inches to be seen beneath the grubby floral print dress which had looked so different on the mail-order catalogue's 'fuller figure' page.

'Can you find the eggs, Mrs Jimson?' she shrilled from the end of the row of shelves to a tall, sensible-looking

woman in sensible brown skirt and jumper, looking down
in a puzzled manner at a trolley whose wheels seemed to
be set permanently in reverse. 'Down by the Omo. See?
That's right. They're nice and fresh, new in day before
yesterday. Will you be wanting sugar then? It's up there
by the meat pastes and things. Yes, isn't it a price, eh? I
don't know what things are coming to, do you? Bit grubby,
you say? Well, it's only the package, isn't it? Can't shift
goods in a town this size, that's the trouble. D'je hear about
Mrs Buller's Val? Didn't you? Well . . .' Here she came a
step or two forward and lowered her voice to a tone three
grades above the choked whisper, Mrs Buller's Val not
being thought worth any greater degree of discretion. 'Well,
she's big again, three months gone, so 'er mother told
Mrs Brewer, that's Mrs Brewer at the fish shop, Eric's
mum, you know, and it's not 'is, not 'er 'usband's, that's
for sure, because Sam Rice wasn't 'ome at the time. 'E's at
sea, y'know, an 'e wasn't 'ome between well before Christmas and last month, not once, so it stands to reason it
can't be 'is – 'less 'e sent it by post, eh? 'Less 'e sent it by
post!'

Here Mrs Leaze, in tribute to her own powers as an
entertainer, burst out into a cackle of laughter that shook
her flabby body up and down in several directions and
rocked several tins of merchandise perilously on the shelves.
Jean Jimson took the opportunity of slipping round to the
next row of shelves, hoping to have heard the last of it,
but Mrs Leaze put a smart stop to her paroxysm and beetled
round at the other end, fearful of a packet of Oxo cubes
being spirited into Mrs Jimson's handbag, because she always said you couldn't trust schoolmasters' wives.

'Tinned peas up there with the marmalades,' she said,
'bit to your right – that's it. Well, as I was saying, it's my
guess 'e's going to accept it as 'is own, because I saw them
lovey-dovey as you like when 'e was 'ome last, an' 'e must've
known then, mustn't 'e? An' it wouldn't be the first time,

either, oh dear me no. Well, that young Peter, the six-year-old, little ginger boy, well, you'd be surprised if I told you 'oo 'is father was. Be more than my life's worth, I can tell you. But 'oo does the 'air put you in mind of, eh? 'Oo does 'e favour? Is that all, love, sure you 'aven't forgotten anything?'

Jean Jimson stuck her trolley firmly against the cash register and said she was quite sure she hadn't forgotten anything. The most irritating part of her visit was now at hand, for Mrs Leaze insisted on broadcasting to the entire shop the item-by-item cost of her purchases, apparently regarding her willingness to do this as irrefutable proof of her own honesty.

'Tin of peas, eighteen pee, frozen fish fingers, that's twenty pee, tin of fish paste – was that a special, love? – well, we'll say ten pee, shall we? bar of chocolate, seven pee . . . 'Ullo, Miss Potts, lovely morning, on your way to the library, were you? Yes, well, I'd fancy a biscuit if I 'ad your job : get a nice packet of lemon-creams to keep yer mind on things. I don't know 'ow you remember all them books, I don't really, you're a marvel . . . Where was I? Pound of New Zealand butter, twenty-five pee, bottle of Cyprus sherry – 'aving guests, are you then? – one pound and five pee . . . That's the lot then, is it? Four pounds, twenty-three pee, isn't it dreadful? 'Ave you got the right, I'm clean out of change today? That's it. Thanks very much, love. 'Ere, did you 'ear about the commercial radio people coming 'ere – I 'ad it from Mrs Withens 'erself . . .'

But Jean Jimson excused herself from hearing about the commercial radio people and Mrs Withens on the grounds that she had left something on to boil. She bundled her bulging bags (one of which promised to burst before she got home) out of the shop, kicking herself for not having bought most of the items three or four pence cheaper last time she was in Barstowe. Before she was well out Mrs Leaze had turned to her other customer, an undersized little person, with a furtive, librarian's expression, and Jean heard her say:

'Did you 'ear about the commercial radio people, then, Miss Potts? No? I'm surprised, you and Mrs Withens being so close. Well, I 'eard it from the lady 'erself . . .'

Destiny is inexorable in a town as tiny as Twytching, and Jean Jimson was fated to hear about Mrs Withens and the commercial radio people before the day was out. When she went to change her library books in the middle of the afternoon, Miss Potts, primly sitting behind her desk and subjecting every title to fierce scrutiny from behind a wicked pair of rimless spectacles, remembered that she had missed the glad tidings.

'Did you like that, Mrs Jimson? Really? Yes, I believe people *do* say she's a good read, but she's not what I'd call a *nice* novelist, is she? She's an Oxford don, so I've heard, so perhaps that explains it. Now I've got the latest Denise Robins. Mrs Carrington brought it back, and she said it's the best Denise Robins she's ever read – and she reads them all, you know: Denise Robins has no more devoted fan than Mrs Carrington. Shall I put it by for you? No, well, please yourself, there's plenty that will.' Miss Potts could not suppress a sigh at the vagaries of human taste as she laid down the Denise Robins. 'You'll find plenty of new things on the shelves: we had a visit from the county people this morning – I haven't had time to go through and see what's there myself yet.'

Jean had timed her visit on the assumption that both these last items of news would be the case – she resented the best things disappearing under Miss Potts's desk as soon as they came in, especially as the casual reader had no means at all of knowing what was there and what was not. While she leafed her way along the shelves, trying to leave them less regimented than she found them, Miss Potts put the inevitable question:

'You didn't hear about Mrs Withens and the commercial

radio people, did you, Mrs Jimson?'

'No,' said Jean. 'Have they asked her to do a commercial for them?'

She idly wondered whether it would be for whale-bone corsets, or a cure for dyspepsia. Miss Potts looked at her reproachfully, as if she had belched during prayers.

'They are coming here,' she said firmly, 'to do a documentary on Twytching, for our American twin town. A sort of *Down Your Way* Mrs Withens said when I rang her. A whole programme on us – just fancy! I'm ever so excited, I can tell you.'

'Do you think you'll be on it, then?' asked Jean, idly thinking it would be difficult to select a more thoroughly uninteresting specimen of the local population than Miss Potts, strong though the competition was.

'Well, of course, Mrs Withens will be on – naturally. And we *are* good friends, what with the library committee, and the Decent Standards League and so on, and I *did* wonder.' Later, as Jean was taking out her chosen books, Miss Potts asked: 'What would *you* choose, Mrs Jimson, as your piece of music?'

'I haven't thought,' said Jean. 'I don't imagine I'll have to choose. What would you?'

'I thought perhaps something devotional. "All in the April Evening" or "Land of Hope and Glory" – something like that.'

'I'm sure everyone would like that,' said Jean.

'It's all in the lap of the gods, of course,' said Miss Potts with a simper. The lap of Mrs Withens, more like, thought Jean. 'Have you found something nice, then? Oh, Angus Wilson! Well, you could almost call him a local, I suppose, couldn't you? Oh, Mrs Jimson! I didn't know this was there. Are you *sure* you want this?'

'Quite sure, thank you,' said Jean.

'Well, you must please yourself, of course. But I always think that people who mock the royal family are the lowest of the low. I'm afraid I think horsewhipping is too good for them. *Good* afternoon, Mrs Jimson.'

And Miss Potts tightened her lips, in a gesture of disapproving dismissal.

It wasn't Jean Jimson's day, because outside the library she met Alison Mailer.

CHAPTER II

ALISON MAILER

Alison Mailer was Jean's next-door neighbour – they lived in almost identical detached houses of some small pretensions on the outskirts of Twytching, if so tiny a town could be said to have outskirts. When she saw Alison coming up the street, Jean's hand went instinctively to her hair, for Alison had the gift of making other women feel they had had a trying day, and were showing it. Sometimes, indeed, she told them directly that they were, for there was little subtlety about Alison. Today, as always, she was looking cool, clean, well-pressed and deadly.

'Jean, lovely to see you,' she said, looking with quite unconcealed contempt at Jean's brown check skirt and chain-store sweater. 'For a neighbour you can be quite a stranger. Where've you just been? Don't tell me you use that pokey little library?'

'Oh, it's not too bad. I don't get that much time to read. In any case, there doesn't seem to be any alternative.'

'We belong to the London Library,' said Alison. 'It's really the only civilized way . . .'

'Have you read anything good recently?' asked Jean maliciously, pretty sure that Alison had hardly opened a book since her schooldays.

'I've just finished the latest Greene,' said Alison, coolly offhand, and clearly about to pass on to another ground for superiority.

'Oh?' said Jean. 'I didn't know Graham Greene had published anything recently.'

'*Henry* Green,' said Alison. 'Of course.'

Jean Jimson racked her brain to remember whether Henry Green was still alive and publishing. She thought not. But you had to hand it to Alison. She managed to pick up all the right names.

'Did you hear about Radio Broadwich?' said Jean as they approached their own front gates.

'Radio Broadwich?' said Alison, bored. 'No. Are those old sex-kittens suing it for playing smutty pop songs?'

'No,' said Jean, unwisely; 'they're coming here, to Twytching. To do a programme.'

'Really?' said Alison, perking up. 'Are you making tea, Jean? You make such a wonderful cup, and I'm dying for a bit of gossip.'

Jean held open the gate with a forced smile, and kicked herself for bringing up such a topic so close to home. When Alison Mailer neglected an opportunity of insinuating herself into prominence, it could confidently be forecast that she was on her death-bed. Now she strolled calmly through the gate and up the path, smiling condescendingly at the rhododendrons, and making it obvious that she registered the weeds in the lawn. Jean let them into the kitchen, and sat Alison down determinedly at the kitchen table, shutting the door on the living-room with its mess of Meccano, half-done jig-saws and hockey-sticks. Alison, who had caught a glimpse, smiled with understanding, and then glanced around the kitchen.

'You don't have many herbs, do you?' she said, her gaze resting on a line of three or four little jars. 'Don't you use them in your cooking?'

'The children don't like them,' said Jean, trying not to grind her teeth. 'And Timothy's not too fond, though he pretends to be.'

'I don't see what they've got to do with it,' said Alison. 'I don't know what I'd do without my little collection.

Anyway, what's this about Radio Broadwich? Have I missed something? Has something been going on here that they could be interested in?'

'Nothing that I know of,' said Jean, slapping too much tea in the pot. 'I'd have heard from Mrs Leaze if there was anything like that – she never misses a trick. No, it's some sort of documentary, for the Americans. You know this twin-town nonsense Mrs Withens has been busybodying herself about. Well, the programme will be sent there, and the local station will broadcast it, and I gather we'll get a chance to hear it first. Apparently it will be a *Down Your Way* type of programme.'

'*Down Your Way*?' said Alison, wrinkling her nose.

'You remember – it's been going for years. They visit a place, and interview people, and play their choice of music – you know the sort of thing.'

'*Really*?' said Alison, her interest now caught. 'And how are they going to choose the people to be interviewed?'

'I've no idea. I expect I'll listen to *Down Your Way* this Sunday, to see what they do. I haven't heard it for years, because Timothy likes quiet for his writing on Sundays. He'll probably want to hear it himself this Sunday, though.'

'Sunday,' said Alison meditatively. 'Radio Four, I suppose. It sounds awfully like Radio Four. I must try and catch it.'

'I imagine they choose people to represent all activities and industries and things in a town,' said Jean. 'And I suppose the Radio Broadwich people will do the same – though God knows, they'll be pushed for material in Twytching. I gather Mrs Withens is already signed up – or she thinks she is,' said Jean. 'And little Miss Potts thinks she's got a chance. Apparently old Mother Withens will be vetting the lists of who should and who shouldn't appear.'

'*Really*?' said Alison again. 'We'll see about that. I can't think why that human dreadnought should have anything to tell the waiting millions. What music do you think she'd choose? "If I Ruled the World"?'

'As far as I can remember,' said Jean, 'that's what most people on *Down Your Way* choose.'

'So I'd imagine,' said Alison, sipping thoughtfully. '*Lovely* tea, Jean, *really* lovely. Have you tried using the filter system, though? I wonder what I'd choose now – as music, I mean . . . something to make people sit up, don't you think?'

Jean decided not to venture on any conjecture of what she might have in mind, for fear of a snub: 'Sit up? How do you mean, exactly?'

Alison thought gracefully.

'What about some Schoenberg, now,' she said finally. 'I wonder what they'd say. Or perhaps some Alban Berg.'

'They'd probably say "no",' said Jean. 'Scrub the interview off the tape and forget you.'

'You've got a point there,' said Alison.

'Still, it's a nice idea,' said Jean. 'I can just imagine how Old Mother Withens would glare next day. Disgracing the fair name of Twytching, and all that. But the point is, there's no question, so far as I can see, of any of us ordinary housewives getting on. Obviously they'll be going for the nobs.'

Alison raised an eyebrow at the 'ordinary housewives', but she merely said: 'There might be ways. You forget, dear, after all, that there *are* no nobs in Twytching. Or if there are, I haven't met them. Do you really *like* those big red spots for a kitchen curtain, Jean? I just ask – I can't quite make up my own mind.'

Alison Mailer walked slowly, meditatively, between Jean Jimson's scruffy, slightly dirty house and her own, her mind half on the approaching descent of the Radio Broadwich Assyrians on the Twytching fold, and half, as usual, complacently meditating on the very obvious differences between her own spotless, sanitized, disciplined dwelling and the dwellings of anyone else in Twytching you would care to name. She looked at the roses, ruthlessly pruned in accordance with the advice of the textbooks and ready for a splendid advance that would turn the neighbours bilious green at the sight of their profusion; she looked at the lawn, evenly cut like a young recruit's poll, not a blade out of place, weedless, punished severely if it strayed on to the paths or beds. How Alison loved watching from her bedroom window the faces which gazed long at her lawn in reluctant, loathing admiration; how she loved being asked how she managed it; how she loved not telling. It was Jean Jimson's contention that the only suitable monument for Alison Mailer, supposing she should ever be obliging enough to die, would be an enormous marble sarcophagus in dubious taste with the words 'the neighbours will be terribly jealous' picked out in gold.

Alison let herself in by her front door, hung her coat up on a hanger in the hall cupboard, and drifted into the lounge, nodding on her way in to her daughter who was doing her homework on the kitchen table. The lounge, like most rooms in the house, had no particular characteristics, except that it was clean and cold – maintaining this last quality quite miraculously, in view of the stiflingly high level at which Alison kept the central heating. The room had been furnished by Alison little by little in the earlier days of her marriage, when money had been much scarcer than it was now, and when her husband had had, sometimes, to deny her things. Each month's *Home Beautiful* had contributed its share to the scheme, and the result was an uneasy mix of tubular-steel-and-leather with bulgy-Victorian, with a substratum of hideous imitation period furniture. The second-rate taste of several generations had gone into the making of the room, and it was no wonder that Alison's daughter preferred the kitchen to do her homework in. Alison looked around the room with a passing dissatisfaction, and sank gracefully (part of her perfection sprang from the fact that she acted, even when quite alone) into the chilly white leather depths of her sofa.

By the time her husband came home, the situation had at least clarified itself in Alison's mind. The first thing that had been decided was that she did indeed want to be interviewed on Radio Broadwich's documentary. It had occurred to her some time after Jean's breaking the news that this programme was unlikely to be an *Akenfield*, that Radio Broadwich was the sort of station listened to mostly by spotty adolescents and the occasional resentful old-age pensioner who couldn't afford a television licence, and that therefore it might be best to stand aside and sneer at the frantic scramblings of everyone else in the town to get on. Mature consideration had persuaded her that it would be still better to be on the programme first and sneer at it afterwards.

This decided, the next step was to resolve that either she *was* on the programme, or else she would have to take a sudden holiday in the South of France at the time of the recording. Or the West Indies. Nothing less would do, if ridicule was to be stifled. Alison was not usually very conscious of what other people thought. She was too wrapped up in her cosy cocoon of egotism and self-satisfaction. But she was conscious that if on this occasion she made determined efforts to get herself on to the programme and then failed, people would laugh at her. Their laughter would spring from their jealousy, of course, she was sure of that, but this was the one side-product of jealousy which she had no desire to bring to birth.

The next step in her thought process was that if she was to be on the programme, she had to find some way of getting on it. It was not going to come along to her front door of its own accord. One possible avenue, of course, was Mrs Withens. That was the avenue most would be taking, and for that reason alone Alison was inclined to shun it. Then again, though Alison had no moral scruples about sucking up to Twytching's Boadicea, she did have doubts (unusually for her) about whether she could manage it successfully. She had once been photographed beside the

Chairman's Lady after the local school prize-giving : even before the picture was taken she had caught Mrs Withens eyeing her tall, svelte elegance as if she regarded it as an invitation to some sophisticated and hardly describable form of sexual activity. Delicious! Alison was confident in her own mind that Mrs Withens kept that picture hidden under her bloomers in her bottom drawer and spent hours comparing Alison's cool grace with her own olive green woolly dress with the lacy neckline, and the dumpy round brown hat, like a failed Yorkshire pudding, with the suspicion of veil drooping down here and there as if uncertain whether to come or go. Perfectly good Twytching wear, of course, but Alison prided herself on having put Twytching wear quietly and eternally in its place. No, it seemed to her that, though she would back herself against Mother Withens any day of the year in a straight fight, nevertheless the old monster was not such a fool as to be deceived by professions of long-intended friendship, by offers of help in some worthy urban enterprise or other, or by vows to stand side by side with her, commanding the waves of public indecency to recede even as they lapped around their chaste ankles.

It would have to be some other way, then. The best thing would be to listen to *Down Your Way* on Sunday, to see what sort of thing was required. She was aware, though, that three and a half thousand people in Twytching would be doing the same thing, of whom something like five hundred would be nourishing firm hopes of themselves putting in an appearance in the Radio Broadwich documentary. However realistic or unrealistic those hopes might be, still the competition would be enormous. Alison liked competition. It was her life-blood. Yet in this case, might it not be amusing to circumvent the opposition? An acorn of a notion fell to the earth of her mind, and a sapling started sprouting. Could it be done? Could it? A cat-like smile of self-approval spread over Alison's face.

By a quarter to seven, when Arnold Mailer came home from his work in London, Alison's daughter, Cressida, had cooked the dinner. Alison went into the kitchen five minutes before he was due in order, as she put it, 'to put the finishing touches' to the meal – in reality to get ready to serve it out the moment he came in the door. She prided herself on always having his meals ready exactly when he needed them; in fact she prided herself on being a good wife to him altogether. And except when her demands for material possessions to match and outstrip any bought by the neighbours drove him over the brink of desperation, Arnold Mailer agreed. He liked women to be decorative and feminine and she was decidedly both; he liked – though he was amiably unconscious of this – he liked women to be able to talk intelligently, but he didn't like them actually to be too intelligent. He told himself, poor fish, that he had a very clever wife. He was a quiet man, infinitely patient, and he saw her for such a small portion of the day that he could put up with her little ways, with her scorn, with her badgering, without the least feeling that he had made anything but a superb bargain in marrying her, without ever once telling himself that he was to be pitied. He was ten years older than Alison, and a clever woman can always give a husband in that position the feeling that she did him a favour by ever considering him in the light of a husband at all. Arnold was duly grateful. When he had finished his beef pizzaiola with the sauté potatoes, had praised the cooking and had had his praise accepted without so much as a glance passing between mother and daughter, he was quite willing to listen to an evening's gossip and conjecture about the approaching visit of the Radio Broadwich team.

'Of course, I seldom hear the radio nowadays,' said Arnold, 'and so far as I know I've never heard Radio Broadwich at all. Heaven knows if they're capable of producing a competent programme.'

'One wonders what the American audience will be expecting,' said Alison.

'Something quaint, something drenched in history, something just a little boring,' said Arnold. 'That would be about their idea of the typical English village.'

'If it's boredom they want,' said Alison, stretching herself elegantly into the chair, 'they shouldn't be disappointed. If Old Mother Withens has her way, though, this will be something extra-special – the greatest mass-switch-off since the days of Mrs Dale.'

'Mrs Withens? Poor old Ernest's wife? Is she going to have anything to do with it?'

'Everything, as far as I can gather. Ernest is Chairman of the District Council at the moment, in case you hadn't registered. So our Deborah is going to vet the lists of who is and who is not to be interviewed – or so Jean Jimson says, at any rate.'

'Maybe, maybe,' said Arnold. 'She may not find it as easy as she thinks, though. I don't imagine these commercial radio chappies kow-tow as much as the BBC.'

'Arnold,' said Alison thoughtfully, 'don't we *know* anyone at Radio Broadwich?'

They both knew perfectly well that none of their mutual friends answered to that description. Such friends as they had were mostly connected with Arnold's construction company, Alison having cast off most of the friends of her youth as insufficiently smart shortly after her marriage. So Arnold rightly took her to mean 'Don't you go up on the train with anyone at Radio Broadwich?' He thought for a bit.

'No, I'm pretty sure we don't,' he said. 'There's Fisher – he's in an advertising firm. He's concerned with the visual side, though, so I don't suppose he'd have much to do with radio.'

Alison allowed a long pause. 'Very helpful,' she said sourly. She looked at the clock, but almost before she did so her daughter had begun collecting up her books. It was the invariable custom of the household that the first spasm of irritation after dinner was the signal for Cressida to be sent to bed.

'Goodness,' said Alison. 'Time for bed, darling. Give Mummy and Daddy a kiss.'

Cressida planted a perfunctory kiss on her mother's cheek and a much more enthusiastic one on her father's. She and her mother seemed to get on excellently. Cressida consented to do much of the housework and cooking in return for being left alone, and not subjected to any of those embarrassing occasional displays of mother love for the benefit of friends or visitors which had embittered her earlier childhood. Neither cared for the other, but they had thus managed to reach an acceptable public *modus vivendi*. Cressida never minded being sent to bed, for she could rely on being left alone to read or write till midnight or beyond – indeed until she fell asleep over her book. This was her idea of paradise.

'If only, Arnold,' said Alison pensively when her daughter had gone, 'if only just *once* in a while you could get to know the right people.'

Arnold Mailer accepted the rebuke meekly.

'I got to know you, after all,' he said. 'That's surely *one* time when I did.'

Alison treated this bit of sickliness with the contempt it deserved.

'God,' she said. She let a moment pass to convey her feelings, and then she continued : 'I wonder about music . . .'

'Music?' said Arnold, not following.

'Music,' said Alison; 'the music I shall choose' – spacing it out as if to a dull child.

'Oh, are you that far already? Well, I don't know – what do you like?'

Alison gave him another withering look.

'That is hardly the point. I thought of Schoenberg or Rodney Bennett or someone like that first – just to annoy Old Mother Withens. But Jean said they'd probably scrub the whole interview, and she may be right for once in her life. What would be the OK names among the older composers at the moment, do you think?'

Her husband was on her wavelength now, and was used to such questions. He pondered for a bit.

'It used to be Vivaldi or Corelli, that sort of figure. Or Purcell, of course. I'm not quite sure who it would be now. Haydn does seem to be very in at the moment, though. Yes – I think you'd be safe in putting your money on Haydn.'

Alison got up from her chair and stretched her shapely length ceiling-wards.

'God, I'm bored with this ghastly little town,' she said. 'I think I'll take a trip to Ipswich tomorrow.'

'Haydn,' said Alison vaguely to the young man behind the counter of the largest music-shop in Ipswich.

'Yes, madam,' said the young man patiently. 'Was it the symphonies you were interested in?'

'That's right, the symphonies,' said Alison, less vaguely.

'Was it the *complete* symphonies you wanted?' asked the young man.

'Of course,' drawled Alison in her most Bond Street voice.

She watched, coolly and impassively aghast, as he went to the shelves and took down boxed set after boxed set after boxed set. Something like a tear of emotion came to the corner of her eyes as she took her cheque-book from her handbag.

Someone's going to pay for this, she thought.

CHAPTER III

JOCKEYING FOR POSITION

It made a change, Jean Jimson thought, not to have to go through Sunday afternoon and evening on tiptoe. The usual pattern after lunch was that her husband would spend half an hour sleeping or having a last flip through the

Sundays, and would then retire to the second bedroom which he used as a study (or 'den', as he called it) for the rest of the day. From then on it was a matter of constantly muffling the children's exuberance, and nothing was more exhausting than that – not even having her husband actually around.

Timothy Jimson was a short, ratty little man whose clothes always hung loosely around him, as if they were giving him plenty of air. He had the appearance of having just recovered from a serious and wasting illness, and his twisted, petulant expression gave colour to this notion. Timothy Jimson was a schoolteacher, and he maintained a precarious ascendency over his pupils by means of tortuous sarcasms which were not the less resented for being only dimly or partially understood. Like any teacher who needed constantly to assure himself of the immense difference in learning between himself and his pupils, he actually taught very little.

Timothy Jimson was also a writer. 'I write,' he would say to people, without any of the customary masks of irony, defensiveness or self-depreciation : 'I write', pure and simple. He had written a clever little play about the Trojan wars, in verse indistinguishable from bad prose, which wittily suggested that the real cause of the wars was not the rape of Helen, but the fall in the commodity prices of copper and wheat. It had been performed to glum little audiences by the Barstowe Players. He had written too for some years a column for the Barstowe paper, which he called 'Twytching Tattle' and signed 'Taper'. He had written ironic fairy stories, with clever twists at the end, and he had been encouraged by the boredom and distaste evinced for them by his own children to collect them and look out for a publisher. At school he was the bore of the common room, having few subjects but himself; at home he was irritable, self-pitying and dogmatic. Jean was a placid type, but she often caught herself, unawares, wondering why she had married him. No reason ever presented itself. She concluded that it was a long time ago, that she had been very young, and that she had much better put the subject out of her mind.

This Sunday, then, was unusual for the Jimsons – and indeed for most of Twytching. People kept telling each other that they 'mustn't forget' what was on at 5.15, and even the children consented to miss their favourite television programmes, though in some cases it needed a mountain of rather disgusting sweets to win their consent to this. The Jimsons went for a little walk, the first in eighteen months, and then sank in to tea and crumpets. At five-ten Jean cleared away. Timothy told Ellen to stop scratching with her crayons, Jeremy to stop banging his Meccano pieces together, and Peter to stop crawling around the floor. Then the whole family settled around the radio set in the sort of frozen immobility that must have greeted Churchill's early war broadcasts, or Edward VIII's abdication speech.

Down Your Way was that week visiting a medium-sized town in the far north of Scotland. Medium-sized towns in the north of Scotland are not, at the best of times, the liveliest of places, and it could not be said that the programme managed to disguise the fact. The compère talked to an amateur archaeologist about the origins of the place, to the star of the local drama group, to the head of the town's WVS, the manager of a local factory making tartan egg-cosies for export, and to someone who designed and produced jewellery, a rather precious gentleman who kept talking about his 'craft' and assuring the interviewer that each piece was 'a unique work of art'. His musical choice was some lyric witterings by Grieg; for the rest it was Kenneth McKellar, Moira Anderson, and various defunct choirs from Luton, Glasgow and the Rhondda valley.

When the programme finished, there was a silence for a few moments in the Jimson household. Jean signalled to the children to go out and play, and then waited to hear what the party line was to be.

'Well,' said Timothy, after a prolonged period of mature consideration, 'so that's the sort of programme they're aiming to send to America.'

'It's very old-fashioned,' said Jean tentatively. 'I didn't know they still made radio programmes like that.'

'You've got to remember, Jean,' said her husband, in his schoolmaster's voice, 'that we get a quite erroneous impression of the States here. Chicago isn't America. Large parts of it are sleepy, old-fashioned, homely places, and if Twytching, Wisconsin, is in that sort of area, I'm sure this type of programme will suit very nicely.'

'True,' said Jean, bored as usual by her husband's habit of expounding his views as if they were a geometrical theorem.

'One hopes that the makers of our programme will try to avoid the element of commercialism that I thought crept into the programme today.'

'Commercialism?' said Jean.

Timothy's face twisted itself into a well-known smile of lordly contempt. 'You mean you didn't notice? Don't you realize that every little squireen within a mile of that place will be ordering something from that jewellery-maker for the lady wife? And you can bet your bottom dollar that the sale of tartan egg-cosies to Hong-Kong will quadruple. Wake up, Jean – it's not like you to be quite so naïve.'

'I suppose you're right,' said Jean, mentally noting that for once he probably was.

'I hope,' said her husband impressively, 'that this documentary on Twytching will not only go deeper into things, but will take a much healthier attitude. Not be so completely materialistic, and concentrate on the things that matter.'

'Well, perhaps,' said Jean. 'But what exactly had you in mind? We don't have a WVS. We don't even do meals-on-wheels for pensioners, so far as I know.'

Her husband sneered. 'Meals-on-wheels!' he said with pregnant scorn. 'I was not thinking of meals-on-wheels, nor Women's Institutes, nor wireless for the blind – nor the whole range of do-goody organizations, nor the whole range of goody-goody organizations . . .'

'What then?' said Jean, feeling fairly sure he had exhausted his limited range of invective.

'Well,' said Timothy, hesitating, and forced at last to bring out over-baldly what had been on his mind all the time; 'there's education, for example.'

Jean was a submissive wife well beyond the calls of duty, but she let this hang in the air several seconds before replying : 'Ye-e-es. Someone at the local school, do you mean? Who would you suggest, then?'

Timothy taught at the grammar school in Barstowe, and she let him digest in silence the idea that this would probably disqualify him from representing Education on *This is Twytching*. Finally he managed to swallow the idea.

'You're probably right,' he said. 'There's no one really. They're a very dim bunch.'

'Not altogether,' said Jean. 'I find Ellen's Miss Marriot very approachable. And there's Jack Edgar.'

This last name was brought out with malice aforethought. Jack Edgar had brought his class to see a performance of *Troy Weight*, Timothy's leaden comedy. He had allowed those who wanted to to leave at the interval, with the result that a great block of thirty-five seats was conspicuously empty out of a total audience of eighty-five.

'Jack Edgar,' said Timothy. 'My God! Skip the idea entirely.'

He sat sunk in gloom for some seconds, his scraggy little hand draped in an artistic pose along his forehead. Jean had noticed that whenever he was thinking about himself as an author he tried to elongate his fingers, as if to make them more artistic. She wondered whether the audience was already at an end and she could get up and do the washing up, but finally he said :

'Of course the arts, if they were approached in an *entirely* non-commercial spirit . . .'

'The arts?' said Jean. 'But who is there? There may be the odd flower-arranger, but I don't know anyone in the village who paints, or sculpts, or makes jewellery.'

'You forget, Jean,' said Timothy Jimson, 'that I write.'

It took Twytching some little time to digest its first taste of *Down Your Way* for at least two decades. Most of the inhabitants had bought television for the present Queen's coronation, which had been the emotional high-spot of most of their lives, and since then had not listened to the radio after half past four in the afternoon. The implications of the programme sank but slowly into the rural brain. This, then, was the sort of programme that was to be made for their American cousins. But what were the lessons for those who aspired to appear? Even Mrs Withens was for a time dubious as to the significance for Twytching of what she had heard, and was troubled. Dubiety was not a state of mind she relished. It had the invariable consequence of making her more aggressive than usual. Thus she was, next morning, particularly hard on her husband as, at ten to seven, he performed the Eileen Fowler Keep Fit exercises in the hall, stripped to his woollen underwear, his face a tense mask of athletic enthusiasm. His endeavours were accompanied by wifely bellows from the bedroom above. 'Stretch,' yelled Mrs Withens when the sprightly Eileen said 'stretch'. 'Higher, higher,' she yelled, to turn the screw harder. But when the sprightly Eileen said 'relax, relax, lower your arms', the voice from the bedroom was silent. Perched as she was in bed, with her cup of tea and marie biscuit resting on her magnificent bosom, Mrs Withens could not see whether or not her husband was actually doing the exercises. She did not need to see. He was doing them.

It was not until a quarter to nine, when she had finished her three-course breakfast and was sitting down to read her daily paper, that the phone rang for the first of many times that morning. It was Mrs Brewer, the local fishmonger's wife, and she wanted to discuss with Mrs Withens, who was, as you might say, the lady mayoress of the town (Mrs Withens nodded gravely into the mouthpiece of the phone) a plan which she had – she said – been turning over in her mind for many months, that of providing meals-on-wheels for all the incapacitated yet deserving pensioners of the town. The scheme conjured up little more in Mrs Withens's mind than a picture of plates with little rollers underneath them, but she lent a gravely interested ear.

'I don't know about you, Mrs Withens dear, but I feel one can't do too much for the senior citizens, provided they are the right *sort* of senior citizen of course, and nobody knows better than myself that the fact that they're incapacitated doesn't mean that they're deserving – far from it often enough, God knows – but I did wonder, you know, whether Twytching hadn't fallen just a *little* behind over the years in that sort of work, not your fault, dear, naturally, but some of us felt that now your good gentleman was chairman we could look to you for a more *energetic* line on what you might call the civic welfare level . . .'

Mrs Withens took advantage of Mrs Brewer taking a short pause for a breath of fishy air to give a snort of modified approval. She approved of welfare services only if the recipients could be proved to be both humble and grateful. An automatic grovel should be the condition of receipt in her opinion.

'Why I'm ringing now,' continued Mrs Brewer, 'was that I *did* hear as how Mrs Buller was on to the same idea, and though I've nothing against her, as you know, nothing against her personally at all, and when you're in business you can't afford to have likes and dislikes, can you, still, well, you'll have heard about her daughter, I suppose . . . yes . . . yes . . . exactly . . . so what I say is it's not a family I'd ever want to have too much to do with, as you say, and one would want our old people to be in the right sort of hands, because a good example goes a very long way, I'm sure you'd agree, Mrs Withens love . . .'

Mrs Withens made noises of conditional assent, and intimated that the matter should have her immediate attention : it suited her power-hungry mind, like any minor civil servant, to keep her petitioners waiting a little in her civic antechambers.

The next call was not in fact Mrs Buller, but Mrs Buller's Val, who said she wanted Mrs Withens's opinion on a little idea she had had : she didn't know if Mrs Withens had noticed, but she was sure she had, that there was very little really for some of the younger women in the village to do, and she'd had the notion of forming a Young Mothers' League, which would meet on . . .

She was interrupted at this point by a thunderous snort from Mrs Withens which shook the telegraph posts, and told her all she needed to know about the reception of her little idea.

In the course of the morning Mrs Withens received telephone calls from Mrs McGregor, the doctor's wife, suggesting that she, Mrs McGregor, should start flower-arranging classes one night a week at the Secondary School, and no doubt Mrs Withens remembered that she had got one first and two seconds at the Barstowe show, not to mention a Highly Commended in the 'Illustrate a Song-Title' class; from June Marriot, an unmarried school-teacher who proposed to remedy the shameful lack of any amateur drama in Twytching; and from Mrs Smith, a woman of no importance who had had a forlorn hope of starting a sewing-bee. In addition, Mrs Buller rang, but her enthusiasm for motorized meals seemed to wane when she heard that she had been forestalled, and finally she said that she *hoped* she *might* be able to help out on one morning a week, but it wouldn't do to count on her. All in all, though, it was a most satisfactory morning, and highly gratifying to Mrs Withens's feelings. She could now be confident that by the time the documentary programme came to be made, Twytching would present the appearance of being quite a lively and thriving little community.

If Mrs Withens's feelings that morning were not unlike those of a Renaissance prince, presiding over the revival of the arts and sciences within his little domain, her afternoon walk gave cause for those feelings to blossom and burgeon to alarming proportions. Her progress through the small town always resembled that of a large liner passing through a narrow strait, but it was not always that the inhabitants of Twytching showed any great enthusiasm for interrupting her passage by exchanging friendly words with her. Privately most people considered that though she was an imposing monument, and a credit to the town, still, personally she was a menace. But today, strangely enough, the eagerness to stop her and to touch metaphorically the hem of one or other of her drab garments was almost universal. Mrs Hopgood told her of her collection of unusual stones and pebbles, picked up throughout the length and breadth of South-East England; Mrs Battersby told her of her clever cat who could open doors; and Mrs Weatherby emerged from the Barstowe bus, cross and panting, her arm through what appeared to be some kind of large wheel which, to judge by the ungainly parcel of brown paper which she was banging against the sides of the bus as she got off, was attached to some sort of frame. Though she was in a state of considerable botheration, Mrs Weatherby brightened up immediately at the sight of Mrs Withens.

"Ullo, Mrs Withens. Didn't know I did my own spinning, did you? And weaving. All the old country crafts. Just tell me any time you might have a use for a length of cloth, and I'll get it done for you in no time.'

It was all very gratifying, to say the least. Mrs Withens did not beam, but she did show some sign of blossoming as she walked home along the streets and avenues, lined with bungalows and semi-detacheds, each with its little front gardens to be inspected and judged as she went. She gave a mental nod of approval to the early daffodils and budding trees, and gave them a good mark for effort. This sunny mood was somewhat tried, alas, by the apparition of the vicar suddenly bursting on to her attention from a side path which led to the bluebell woods and tottering in her direction as fast as his rickety old legs would allow, his head going spastically in this direction and that, and his once-red hair now like a disorder of sun-drenched corn. Mrs Withens knew that once he got that speed up, there was little danger of his stopping, but he slowed down a fraction, raised his right finger in a gesture of blessing and in his astronomically high voice and old-fashioned accent said :

'Blessings on you, Mrs Withens, and on your good husband – on your risings in the morning and on your goings to bed at nights. Blessings on you . . . blessings . . .'

And before Mrs Withens had had time to do more than bend her head briefly, the minimal acknowledgement of a Lord Temporal to a Lord Spiritual, he was gone down the road with a manic chuckle and a frantic nodding of the head. As usual after such encounters, Mrs Withens wondered whether she ought to write to the bishop. Four years now he had been like that, and it seemed idle to expect that anyone in the church would notice, let alone actually do anything about it.

Her ruffled spirits were a little soothed as she walked on when she saw that Inspector Parrish was in his garden. If the Church was unworthily represented in Twytching, the Law, in her opinion, was not. Such a nice man – the image of the dependable, slow-thinking, right-minded type that ought to administer law and order in such a community. A lovely garden he had in summer, too, though perhaps a little too unregimented for her taste. The very best type of man, nevertheless. She would throw a word in his direction as she passed.

Inspector George Parrish had kept himself in Mrs Withens's good graces during his five years' residence in Twytching by dint of listening, nodding and hiding his feelings. If he thought her a ridiculous old cow, and he did, he also knew that a good policeman does not wantonly reveal his opinion of any law-abiding citizen, and more especially not of such a pillar of the community as Mrs Withens. The reticence necessary to the job had always been one of its main attractions for him, for he liked with strangers to keep his counsel, not to be forced out into the open. He was to all intents and purposes a slow, kindly, rather slovenly countryman. His uniform never looked over-smart, and his sports jackets did not go over-often to the dry cleaner's. He was a bachelor, used to fending for himself, and using up all his surplus energies in his garden. He had a large collection of records, and enjoyed a quiet pint in the Lamb and Child, provided it was not accompanied by too much politics thank you very much. Everyone said, condescendingly, that George Parrish wasn't much of a talker. No one ever said that he was a very good listener, and some of them would be just a little uneasy if they had realized just how good a one he was. There was little or nothing that had gone on in Twytching in his five years' residence that was not stored in his mind, and cross-referenced there to boot, but the inhabitants of the town, hugging their nasty little secrets, would have been willing to bet that George Parrish thought of little when he was off duty but roses and gladioli. With his sergeant, in the privacy of the station, he could be caustic and expansive, but otherwise he limited his outward emotions to quiet interest and sympathy. Whatever else took place in his mind, took place behind his eyeballs. Thus, behind his eyeballs he was cursing as Mrs Withens approached, looking the very image of a pillar of the community, and one no Samson would lightly take on the demolition of, cursing that he had not unbent himself from his weeding and registered her approach earlier, so that he might decently have disappeared round the back with a wheelbarrow of rubbish. But his eyes showed only a mild welcome as she wheeled her stately bulk around and addressed him over the wall.

'A lovely day at last, Inspector,' said Mrs Withens, who

invariably gave him his title.

'Indeed, ma'am,' said Parrish. 'Just the day I've been waiting for, and lucky I am to have the day free to use it.'

The hint was lost on Mrs Withens, as hints always were. If she had something to discuss with the Inspector, discuss it she would, and without any fussy preliminaries if necessary.

'The vicar,' she said bluntly, 'is getting worse.'

'You don't say so?' said Parrish. 'Ah well, that's a shame, now. Poor old gentleman.'

'Pity is all very well,' said Deborah Withens, whose stocks of that commodity were always low and diminishing, like winter coal, 'but he is the spiritual leader of this community, one must think of that. The possibilities are frightening to contemplate.'

Inspector Parrish thought that there was very little difference between a clergyman in possession of all his faculties and a clergyman in possession of none of them, since in the context of modern village life both were equally irrevelant and ineffectual. The difference between a good vicar and a poor vicar could, in his opinion, be measured by the takings at a church bazaar. But these were not thoughts to be aired in the presence of Mrs Withens, and he merely said :

'You're right there, ma'am. Could be awkward if things were allowed to go too far.'

'I meditate writing to the bishop,' said Mrs Withens. 'But there again, if I were to do that, could I confine myself to the vicar? There is so much in this little community that by rights a bishop should be aware of, as you no doubt know only too well, and it may be that this is not quite the time . . .'

'What kind of thing was it you had in mind, then?' asked Inspector Parrish unwisely, as she faded into a loaded silence.

'The sort of thing, Inspector, that doesn't come within your domain, more's the pity, but would if things were properly ordered. The children born out of wedlock, or as good as. The men who consort with other people's wives. The unnatural vice!'

Inspector Parrish was privately of the opinion that there was very little sleeping around in Twytching, and he had even wondered whether it might not be a happier little community if a bit more did. A more lethargic and conformist town would be hard to find this side of the iron curtain, and most of the energies which might have gone into sex in fact went into tittle-tattle, back-biting and petty conspiracy. He knew that most of the men loved their cars infinitely more than any other human being. He certainly didn't think for one moment that the bishop would be surprised by anything that Mrs Withens could find to tell him.

'We've got our plates pretty full in the force as it is,' he said dryly. 'We'd have to have a recruiting drive before we took on that kind of thing as well.'

'True, true,' said Mrs Withens, giving every appearance of taking this point in all seriousness; 'but no doubt with improved pay and conditions . . . But, as I say, I doubt if this is the time. As you have no doubt heard, we are being visited by Radio Broadwich. This is not the time to wash dirty linen in public. I intend to see that we put our best foot forward! Both our best feet, in fact!'

'Very gratifying for the village as a whole, that,' said the Inspector. 'There'll be a lot of interest, I doubt.'

'Yes, very gratifying for the town,' said Mrs Withens, with a slight emphasis on the noun, for Twytching had something near four thousand inhabitants, and Mrs Withens took the view that if you diminished Twytching, you diminished her. 'Interest, of course, there will be,' she continued, swelling visibly and unpleasantly, 'and it is to be welcomed if it is interest of the right kind. Many have already spoken to me about appearing on the programme, though they do not put it in so many words. There is no doubt a good deal of conspiring going on, and a good deal of talk. But people will have me to deal with, and you can be sure I shall not be easy to "come over". I intend that the Americans shall get a healthy, edifying picture of our little community, and I am not to be fooled into letting through anyone who is unworthy of us in any way.'

The woman seemed more ridiculous and more nasty by the minute, and even someone as reticent as Inspector Parrish felt the need to give her a word of warning.

'Very commendable, ma'am,' he said, 'but if you'll allow me to say so, rather dangerous. These little towns can be full of little unpleasantnesses under the surface, and if once they're stirred up, nasty things can happen – things which I *would* be interested in, as a policeman. If I were you, I'd leave it to the gentleman producing the programme to decide who will or won't be on it. That way, you see, there won't be anyone in Twytching for people to – well, to focus their discontent on to, like.'

It was a long speech for Inspector Parrish, but it was followed by a silence almost equal in duration. Mrs Withens was disappointed in him, and this was her method of letting him know it. What was more, he had struck a blow at her own image of herself. When she spoke, it was with magisterial emphasis.

'I'm sure you mean well, Inspector,' she said. 'But when I shrink from my duty, then I shall know that the time has come for me to lay down the burdens of office. That time has not come yet. Not quite yet.'

Far from shrinking, she seemed still more to be swelling minute by minute. She bent her head in displeasure towards the inspector, changed her tack, and proceeded in the direction of home with the storm-clouds gathering ominously around her head. Leave it to the producer of the programme! Preposterous! No one who knew anything of the force and determination of her personality, her splendid consistency of purpose, would imagine anything of the kind to be possible. And as for stirring up ill-will in the community – when had she shrunk from such a stirring when necessary? There were, in fact, many of her fellow inhabitants to whom she had long been intending to give a piece of her mind, without having yet found the occasion. She had no doubt that in the course of the next few weeks, those occasions would present themselves.

In fact, she was in the midst of this moral meditation when she saw approaching in the distance, from the direction of the Methodist Chapel, just such a one as she had been thinking of. In a moment she was restored to something like equanimity. Mrs Mailer! Alison Mailer, of the cool, fashionable clothes! Alison Mailer of the supercilious expression! If there was anybody Mrs Withens would like to believe was sleeping around it was Alison Mailer : why else would she look so coolly inviting after twelve or thirteen years of marriage? It wasn't in nature. What a pity she had no evidence of any sexual escapades of this sort. Perhaps she had a *pied-à-terre* in London. Mrs Withens savoured the amorous connotations which gathered in her mind around that undoubtedly un-English phrase. Yes, her extra-marital adventures must take place in a *pied-à-terre*!

And here she was, coming towards her, and without a doubt itching to get on *This is Twytching*. Alison Mailer was a pusher, if ever Mrs Withens saw a pusher. Of course she would stop and speak to her, as everyone in Twytching had stopped to speak to her that afternoon. And what little hobby would Mrs Mailer have invented to press her claim to represent the best in Twytching? Would she suggest forming a branch of the WI? Or perhaps starting fashion classes in the evening? Or did she dabble in watercolours? The prospect of worsting her was glorious. Deborah Withens tensed her muscles and clothed herself from head to toe in that ice of disapproval and negation with which she intended to meet any such proposal. In a moment she would reach the spot where she calculated Alison would have visibly to notice her, put on a false smile of friendship, and start across the road to accost her.

But Alison came to that spot, and passed it. She continued on her cool, graceful way without apparently feeling the need to cross the road and pay her respects to the symbol of civic government proceeding in the opposite direction. So that all that happened was that just before they passed each other Alison gave Mrs Withens a distant, studied wave and a smile of gracious condescension, while her eyes strayed as if involuntarily and with infinite contempt in the direction of Mrs Withens's sensible walking shoes. And in a moment she was gone.

Deborah Withens felt blow through her a cold wind of fury, a spasm of balked revenge. Someone would pay for this: even if it was only Ernest, someone would pay.

CHAPTER IV

RADIO BROADWICH

The chain of events that had led to the memorable day on which the letter had arrived on Mrs Withens's breakfast plate had many links, and one of the most vital of those links had been an incident on the previous visit to Twytching of Ted Livermore, Features Producer for Radio Broadwich. At 12.45 on Sunday, January 27th, Joy Billington, landlady of the Lamb and Child public house, had leant forward, resting her succulent breasts on the bar top and pointed them invitingly in the direction of the only person in the bar whose face she was not familiar with, saying: 'Haven't seen you here before, love. Have you just come to live round here, then?' The stranger was Ted Livermore, and it was at that moment that he decided he would be coming back to Twytching.

Ted was a native of Barnsley, and a second-class graduate in Sociology from Leicester University. His father had

worked in the Town Clerk's office, and his mother did three
mornings a week in a dress shop, wore her skirts too short
or too long, and tried to talk with a Southern accent. Ted
was stocky, randy in an undiscriminating sort of way, and
inclined to melancholy. He was the sort of person who
went through life looking as if he was wearing his brother's
trousers. He had seen through Sociology in his second term
of study, but he had never summoned up the energy to
change subject. Previous to his coming to Broadwich, he
had been employed by the BBC. He was an unlikely em-
ployee of the BBC – he knew it, and everybody else knew
it. He had in fact been recruited in the early years of Lord
Hill's reign, when the idea had suddenly been put around
that for a public corporation the BBC engaged its staff
on much too much of an old-boys-together, pansier-than-
thou basis, and that something more democratic was
called for. This was also in the days of the first Wilson
government, when several spurious gestures had been made
in the direction of greater democracy by a number of
official and semi-official bodies. The matter had become a
common subject of tea-time chatter in BBC canteens. 'What
we need is a few provincial mediocrities,' a high executive
had been heard to say, with a little giggle. The policy had
not lasted long, and Ted Livermore had found himself
stranded, a fish out of water, a plastic mac in a world of
Jermyn Street shirts and leather shoulder-bags. He kept
telling himself it was a good job, that he'd be a fool to
chuck it in, and probably his habitual lethargy would have
prevented him ever making a move if the offer from
Radio Broadwich, made through the boy-friend of a girl-
friend of his, had not coincided with the rejection by his
immediate superior of his second suggestion for a *Book at
Bedtime*. Ted had a sudden feeling that he didn't wish to
work for an organization with such odd ideas of what was
and was not suitable for such a spot, and he handed in his
resignation. The next day he sat around waiting for some-

one to beg him to withdraw it. Some weeks later he moved to Broadwich.

At the moment when Joy Billington thrust her remarkable pectoral proportions under his thirsty gaze he was returning from what had been intended as a dirty weekend at Walton-on-Naze with a virginal young temp from Aberdeen. At the last moment she had gone all Scottish on him, and had taken the train back to Broadwich in floods of apologetic tears, leaving him to the sea-birds and the tea-rooms closed during the winter months. Thus he was just in the mood for Mrs Billington's air of general availability, and he replied : 'Just passing through. But I'll be back.' In spring, he thought. When the sap is rising.

One of his first programmes with Radio Broadwich had been just such a documentary made for an Essex village with a twin in Canada. It had been stupendously tedious, for Ted, in his infinite lethargy, had let all the local bigwigs shoulder their way into the act. The powers-that-be at Radio Broadwich had told him it was a damned bad programme but a damned good idea. There might be money in more link-ups like that, and money was something Radio Broadwich was not getting enough of. Thus, when the talk turned on that January day in the Lamb and Child to the matter of the twin towns scheme (which was widely ridiculed), Ted's mind was made up. He contacted the Wisconsin station, and everything else flowed naturally from there.

The memory of Mrs Billington's various charms (she drew a good pint as well) had perhaps become a mite less vivid by early April when, in reply to his formal note to the chairman of the District Council telling them that the joint venture with the Wisconsin station had been set up, and that they would be arriving in Twytching in May, he had received Mrs Withens's magisterial reply. He'd had such letters when he set up the previous programme, but whereas they had been transparently interested offers of assistance Mrs Withens's letter read more like a royal summons to the presence, or a Papal Bull. If she was allowed to get a grip on the programme, his credit at Radio Broadwich would sink to zero.

'Screw her,' said Ted Livermore, as he threw the letter back on to the pile on his chaotic desk.

'Who's that, darling?' said the Assistant Features Producer, with whom he shared an office, pausing in the process of nail-filing, and fluttering a delicate eyelash in his direction.

'This old cow,' said Ted, looking with distaste at the aggressively dyed orange hair, the necklace of chunky beads and the lavender slacks. He asked himself for the hundredth time why the big-wigs at Radio Broadwich had had to wish this thing on him. When there were plenty of others who'd be grateful, too. What he wouldn't do for a nice lazy day to himself in the office. A real feet-up-on-the-desk day. Suddenly a brainwave struck him.

'Perhaps,' he said, 'this is the sort of situation that requires personal contact. Yes – someone should go down and talk to the old bitch. I think this is a job for you, Harold.'

'Yes, I couldn't agree with you more, Mrs Withens darling,' said Harold Thring next day, prancing nervously up and down the living-room of Glencoe. 'I'm with you every teeniest step of the way. But you've got to understand the position.'

Mrs Withens, who at her best resembled a frog of the least companionable kind, had acquired in the course of this brief interview with the representative of Radio Broadwich a vulpine look, like Clytemnestra on one of her difficult days. She had hardly been able to bring herself to invite him into the house, until she realized what people would say if they saw her talking to him on the front doorstep. Now she averted her eyes from the orange hair, specially permed for the trip, and contented herself with looking daggers at the lavender slacks while she waited for 'the position' to be explained.

'We have done this sort of show before,' said Harold, with a brilliant smile in her direction, 'and we're hoping to do more, and make quite a money-spinner out of them. And Ted has taken the view that if we always have the Mayor and the Chairman, and the Squire and so on – or even if we have their charming ladies – the whole thing does become just a tiny *weeny* bit predictable. We're going to keep these shows bright as a button, and each one different! We take the view that it takes all sorts to make a village, to coin a phrase, and we're going to get *all* those sorts on to our programme. So though our producer will want to *talk* with you, quite informally, to get the atmosphere, the feel of the place as it were, I do *rather* doubt whether he'll decide to interview you, actually on the air, as it were.'

There was a heavy silence.

'I see,' said Mrs Withens.

'You'll like Ted,' pursued Harold. 'He's a lovely boy. You'll get on like a house on fire, I just know.'

Mrs Withens felt able to make no promises of combustion on her part. She felt a deep pain in her bowels which any competent physician could have diagnosed as thwarted ambition. Her instinct was to rise from her chair, seize this painted gentleman and tear him apart, limb from limb, as she very well could, even though she didn't do the Eileen Fowler exercises. All that prevented her was the thought of how great would be her overthrow in Twytching estimation if it were known that she and the powers-that-be at Radio Broadwich had come to a violent parting of the ways. Better, much better to let people think her power was as great as they had hitherto assumed it to be. So she watched in silence as Harold Thring drew a beringed hand through his Seville orange hair. Then, when he had worked himself up into a quivering lather of nervous excitability, she intoned : 'I have drawn up a list. A list of the inhabitants of Twytching who in my opinion would be suitable for interview.'

'Have you, dear?' said Harold. 'Super! Fabulous! Well, we'll be doing our own little bit of homework in the area – oooh!' He paused in his perambulations around the room to admire a pastel-blue figurine of a ballet dancer, female of course. 'Pretty, ever so pretty – well, as I was saying, we'll be making our decisions in the next few weeks, then perhaps we could compare lists. That would be fun, wouldn't it? And of course we may find that you, with your local knowledge and all, have found some really *lovely* people that we missed, and that will be awfully grateful-making.'

The idea that she was being given a total brush-off got through but slowly to Mrs Withens.

'Then you do not wish to go through my list now,' she said in her most Mrs Siddons voice.

'Much more jolly later on,' said Harold, picking up a little brass bell from the mantelpiece. 'Oh – tinkle-tinkle!'

'In fact you intend to ignore altogether the leaders of Twytching, the best elements in the community?'

'It's not a question of *me*, Deborah ducky,' said Harold, flashing a choir-boy's come-hither look in her direction. 'If it was a question of me, I'd interview you like a shot, really I would. It's just a question of the programme, and the policy laid down. And if Ted says we avoid councillors and mayors and things, he's boss, and what he says goes.'

Mrs Withens had been called Deborah ducky, and the heavens had not fallen in. Mrs Withens thought she might be forced to revise her opinion of the heavens. Her soul screaming with shame at having to petition for information, she made a last attempt to winkle out the intentions of this odious Ted, so that she could at least make a show of being in his innermost counsels:

'May I ask who, then, you intend to interview, if I may be taken into your confidence to that extent?'

'That's just what we don't know yet, darling,' said Harold, brightening up now that Clytemnestra seemed to have gone on to the defensive and showed signs of being about to bring the interview to a close. 'As I say, we intend to be unpredictable. Footloose and fancy-free, that's us. I'll be going around today having a high old time – talking to everybody, quizzing into every little thing. All the village traditions, all the things you've been doing from time imm. All the hobbies and oddities, all the clubs and pubs. Just so I've got the *feel* of the place, the *whiff*, you might say. Then when I get back to Broadwich I'll brief Ted, and then he'll be down on the actual week to do some more scouting, and he'll take the final decision. Did I tell you what a lovely boy Ted was? Oh, I did. Well, we're a marvellous team, him and I. We're Features, you know. We go very deep into the places we visit. We're a thorough pair, I do assure you.'

Mrs Withens gave him a baleful look intended to assure him that she would not dispute *that* fact, and got up.

'Then,' she said, 'if you decline to accept my advice, if you refuse to pay attention to those best suited to guide you on community matters, I have nothing further to say. Nothing at all. This is, in fact, exactly what I should have expected from a commercial radio station, and I blame myself for not having foreseen it. We shall see, Mr . . . Mr Thrrrring, but when I think of the sort of account I fear you are only too likely to give of Twytching, I shudder – I shudder to the very marrow of my bones!'

And she shuddered accordingly, and showed him majestically to the lead-lighted front door, with its elaborate pattern of tulips and daffodils on a violet background.

'Nice,' said Harold, touching it appreciatively, 'ever so handsome.' And he pranced down the front path, waving gaily, and telling himself that he had got off a lot better than he had first expected. The front door shut behind him with an Ibsenite finality.

Harold, tripping delicately round in his Italian shoes, had a lovely day after that. From the moment he had arrived in Twytching and asked the way to Mrs Withens's, he had been marked down as an emissary from the world of mass communications. 'When I saw the purple trousers I thought 'e might be a new curate,' said Mrs Leaze to Miss Potts, leaning confidentially over the cash register, 'but when I saw the eyelashes, I knew it must be Radio Broadwich!' Thus he was accosted, flattered, and bombarded with information, invitations and self-advertisements. He basked in the sort of popularity which had not been his since his first years at public school. He tasted innumerable home-baked scones, admired innumerable babies and herbaceous borders, and drank endless toasts to Twytching in little glasses of cloudy home-made wine. When the day ended he made himself a nook in an ever so cosy corner of the Lamb and Child, and even there he found himself so much the centre of attention that one after another of the locals came over to have a chat and buy him a gin and tonic. 'I'll do the same for you when my ship comes in,' said Harold. And in the rare intervals when he was left alone, he enjoyed himself enormously gazing doe-eyed at the manly form of Tom Billington, a stalwart cockney, born to the hotel-trade, ex-part-time wrestler and the heftiest pump-arm in the business. One way or another, it seemed likely that the name of the Lamb and Child would soon become familiar to the inhabitants of Twytching, Wis.

Ted Livermore's quiet day in the office was not as idyllic as he had hoped. Though nominally Features Producer, he was, like everyone else in the harum-scarum world of Radio Broadwich, jack-of-all-trades, and called on to do anything and everything at short notice, from announcing programmes to threading typewriter ribbons for incompetent secretaries. So in the course of the morning he did a bit of interviewing, a bit of disc-jockeying, said 'Super' a dozen or so times, and then settled down for a snooze over *The Times* crossword. But, in fact, he had dozed for no more than twenty minutes when he was aroused by a tap on the door. When he had snorted and shaken the sleep out of his head, and when he had sat himself up against the desk as if in the process of writing a letter, he was forced to shout 'Come in'.

It was a tall, elegant figure that met his eyes, the sort of woman that city dirt never seems to dirty, a coolly perfect creature.

'Is it Mr Livermore?' she said with a smile of deep personal interest in the matter.

Ted nodded and gestured towards the armchair.

'You're going to produce *This is Twytching*, aren't you? Charles told me to come along and see you.'

'Charles?' said Ted.

'Sir Charles Watson. He owns the *Barstowe Gazette*. I think he's your principal shareholder too, isn't he? My name is Mailer, by the way – Alison Mailer.'

CHAPTER V

A CONCERN FOR THE AMENITIES

It was not generally known that Twytching had a Town Amenities Protection Group. Mrs Withens knew, because Mrs Withens knew everything. Miss Potts knew, because she had had to send to the County Library for various old maps which might (but did not) illuminate controversial matters concerning boundaries and rights of way. But the vast majority of the inhabitants of Twytching were unaware of the Amenities Protection Group, and might even have been hard put to it to name many amenities, let alone any that needed protection. Which suggested that few of them read 'Twytching Tattle' in the *Barstowe Gazette*, for Timothy Jimson had given the group a great deal of publicity in his column. Not surprisingly, since he himself was the founder, and one of the very few members of the group.

Timothy had had the idea of forming such a pressure group when a local farmer had threatened to enclose totally a field near the Jimson home. Timothy was in the normal way no great lover of nature, thinking of himself as an eighteenth-century figure (Pope or Swift, of course, with his family and friends as dunces or Lilliputians) and therefore above the irrational excesses of the Romantics. On the other hand, his children were accustomed to use a foot-path across this field to get to the track leading to the bluebell woods – a favourite spot for children and courting couples, who found it difficult enough to get any privacy away from the prying eyes of Twytching gossips. And Timothy was accustomed to sending his children to the bluebell woods as often as possible at weekends and during the long summer evenings, to get them out of his artistic hair. Thus he worked himself up into a tremendous lather in his column over a space of several weeks, talking a great deal of nonsense about rights of way and common land from time immemorial. From this it had been but a short step to discovering two or three other burning issues such as the design of the new street lighting and the provision of seats for old people, and then calling a public meeting to discuss these and related topics. Six people had turned up to the meeting, two of them old-age pensioners who went to anything where the room was likely to be heated. A committee of three had been formed, consisting of Timothy, Miss Marriot, the local primary-school teacher who had recently displayed an interest in drama, and Alison Mailer, who could never bear to be left out of anything that might get her talked about. Timothy had done a bit of research into public footpaths, with the help of little Miss Potts, but after a month or two the farmer had changed his mind for agricultural reasons (government policy having changed yet again), and Timothy had been able to hail this in his column as a great victory for public spirit and civic awareness. The Amenities Protection Group had been promptly forgotten.

It was doubtless entirely by coincidence that, as Chairman of the Group, Timothy decided to call a public meeting on the Monday of the week in May that Radio Broadwich's *This is Twytching* was to be recorded. No one could appear more blithely unaware than he that the producer of the programme and his assistant would be in Twytching the whole of that week, but in fact this was one of the little gobbets of information which Mrs Withens had let fall after Harold Thring's visit to reinforce people's opinions that she and the gentlemen from Broadwich were hand in glove in this matter, and that no step would be taken without her express sanction.

On the subject of who was to be on the programme Mrs Withens was playing her cards very close to her capacious bosom, and had caused a good deal of resentment and confusion thereby. For the most part she kept silence, but occasionally she made remarks of a nature so gnomic that people would shake their heads and say that Mrs Withens was a deep one and no mistake, and sometimes add that one day she would go too far. Her conduct caused particular concern to her closest friends and allies, who had expected by now explicit confirmation of their being the elect and chosen of the Lady. Little Miss Potts had cried tears more copious than usual into her Denise Robins as she sat in bed at night and sipped her Ovaltine. Her hopes had been high, and her musical choice had finally been made (a piece from *Swan Lake,* which seemed to her cultural without being aggressive), and now Deborah would speak on the subject only in riddles. It is thus that great leaders are accustomed to test the loyalty of their most devoted followers.

So when Timothy called his public meeting, the public uncertainty on the position and intentions of Mrs Withens ensured a good deal more interest and enthusiasm than had existed on the last occasion. Just as Timothy himself felt that this was the ideal way to reinforce his already high claims as a writer, so most of the inhabitants of Twytching felt that there was just a chance that they might by-pass the iron maiden (the current favourite description of Mrs Withens) and make direct contact with the producer or his rather strange deputy. And among the silent mass of Twytchingites there was a curiosity to see and recognize the gentlemen from Radio Broadwich which reports about Harold Thring's visit had done nothing to quench.

There was one surprising absentee. Timothy had sent a note to Alison Mailer, in her capacity of Committee Member of the Amenities Protection Group, telling her of his intention of calling the meeting, and he had been considerably surprised to receive a note a few days later saying that she was unavoidably prevented by business from attending, and wishing the meeting every success. Timothy had racked his brains to think of the motive behind this refusal. He didn't know much about people, but he knew enough about Alison Mailer to know that she would move heaven and earth to get a spot on *This is Twytching*. And here she was throwing up a first-rate chance of impressing her elegant self on the mind of the producer. Strange indeed. What the 'business' which prevented her attending could be, Timothy puzzled greatly over. There was nothing else on in Twytching that night he was quite sure (there never *was* anything on in Twytching at night). Alison Mailer was only an occasional visitor to London, and when she went she went to swap patronage with the shop assistants of the better stores, and to walk up Bond Street looking as if she couldn't quite decide how to invest her spare millions. Otherwise, as far as Timothy knew, Alison *had* no business. It was all very puzzling.

He thought of co-opting Jean, his wife, on to the committee for the evening, but he decided it might make the meeting look too much of a put-up family affair, and he didn't want to pay a baby-sitter, so he left her at home. On the platform of the primary school hall sat only himself and June Marriot, the leader of the newly-formed Twytching Thespians, a pretty little rosebud thing who on this occasion gave the impression that all she wanted to do was fade into the background of dirty beige and green-painted walls. But if the platform was thin, in the body of the hall, to compensate, there were no less than seventy souls, which surely must have been something of a record for public meetings in Twytching. There had been less when Mr Heath appeared at an election meeting. Considerably less.

The audience turned up in little knots and flurries between half past seven and a quarter to eight. The meeting was called for eight, but since they had only come to chat and look, most people gave themselves plenty of time beforehand. Mrs Leaze shuffled in in her splendid musquash, bought on her inflated profits, though the grand effect was somewhat marred by the expanse of grubby petticoat showing underneath.

'What's it all about then, eh, Mrs Brewer?' she shrieked to the fishmonger's lady, who was taking time off from her disinterested endeavours to provide a meals-on-wheels service. 'I don't know what they mean by amenities, all these new words, do you? Strikes me if a village shop i'n't an amenity, I don't know what is, eh?' She crowed with merry laughter. 'Same with fishmongers, of course.'

Miss Potts crept in, and sat in a corner seat right at the back of the hall. Her eyes were in her lap, but she was watching everyone out of the corner of those eyes, just as she had trained herself to keep the whole of her little library under surveillance from her seat at her desk. She tut-tutted as loudly as she dared when Mrs Buller sailed in, with her Val in tow, already almost aggressively pregnant and dressed in a fluorescent green garment. Val's sailor husband followed them, chunky and sheepish and giving every sign of having been dragged along. Jack Edgar from the secondary school, Timothy's *bête noire,* strolled in and lounged across two seats in the back row, his face set in an expression of tolerant patronage of anything Timothy could put on. He knew that if the Radio Broadwich men came they would sit at the back, and with Miss Potts blocking one end, he thought it a fair bet that they would take the other if it were vacant. Therefore he sprawled his length across the fifth and sixth seats in, and gave no welcoming looks to anyone who might feel like sitting with him.

Mrs Withens arrived a minute or two later. No back row for her. She chugged up the side gangway making grave acknowledgements to various nervous little greetings. She eased herself gently down into her seat in the third row, with a sense on her of the absurdity of any public occasion in which she did not play a major role. She drew her fox fur around her and tried to look benign. Arnold Mailer slipped in late, and took a seat towards the back, perhaps feeling that he had to put in an appearance since his wife was neglecting her duty. None of these local notables were what the public had come to see, however. At one minute to eight Ted Livermore slouched apologetically into the hall, followed by Harold Thring, who could not enter a room apologetically to save his life. They looked around them, Ted with every appearance of wishing himself at any other of the earth's dead ends, and made for the back row as Jack Edgar had known they would. Timothy Jimson had his equilibrium upset by seeing Jack Edgar acknowledge them with just the right degree of friendly but not cringing interest, and most of all by seeing the greeting returned – in the case of Harold with some suggestions of personal interest. His equilibrium was further upset a moment or two later, when he was just clearing his throat to begin and setting his face in an unaccustomed expression of welcome and benignity, by the vicar, who entered the hall in a disorder of arms and legs, flailing his way up the gangway and upsetting several empty chairs in his path. Finally he stationed himself in front of the centre of the stage and cleared his throat for silence :

'Blessings be on this meeting,' he shrilled, peering up at the rafters in a short-sighted manner, 'and God's grace be on the tasks you set yourselves. Evil is at work among us,'

he continued dramatically. Several in the audience looked
guiltily into their laps. Miss Potts, Mrs Withens and a few
others looked straight ahead, guilty of no greater evil than
self-righteousness, complacency and lack of charity. 'Evil
is here, with us, at work in slander, in rumour-mongering,
in the propagation of lies. Put out all evil counsellors, set
not Mammon upon the seat of righteousness, nor worship
the works of the ungodly. Humble thyselves to His com-
mands and the Lord will bless thy comings and thy goings,
thy couplings and thy uncouplings. Through Jesus Christ
our Lord, Amen.'

And he was gone by a side-door, knocking over a lectern
on his way, before the meeting could recover itself from
its posture of semi-reverence and semi-ridicule. Used as
Timothy Jimson was to the sight of the vicar exposing his
second-childishness to the village, it was undeniable that
he was a difficult act to follow. He could think of nothing
more striking to do than to stand up and say: 'Well, perhaps we'd better begin, then.'

This said, he indulged in the usual orator's tricks while
the hall stilled itself from its mutterings and giggles over
the conduct of the vicar, and launched into an opening
speech which he had been preparing for some weeks. As a
starting-point, he touched with a becoming modesty which
deceived nobody on the victory achieved since the last meeting in the matter of Three-Bottoms Field (a name he had
discovered in his Records Section research, and one which
totally mystified everyone in the hall, though Harold
thought it sounded attractive). He passed from this to the
matter of seats for old-age pensioners in the main street,
touching gracefully as he did so on the splendid meals-on-
wheels service being provided for the same, and the sterling
work being put in by Mrs Brewer and her devoted body
of helpers. Mrs Brewer sat there glowing modestly, and
looking forward longingly to the day when the whole thing
could be dropped.

Then Timothy passed on to the other matters he had been

thinking up over the past weeks, and launched himself into
the inexhaustible topic of the need for a community hall
and centre, with special reference to the needs of the
dramatic society. This involved a convoluted tribute to his
blushing fellow committee member, whose notion the
dramatic society had been, and a long recital of the endless
possibilities for fund-raising – bazaars, sweepstakes, special
appeals and various forms of genteel blackmail. By this
stage Timothy was speaking quite well. Any teacher, other
than the most hopeless and tongue-tied, can summon up
a reasonably convincing flow of mellifluous nothings for
an occasion of this sort, which is no doubt one reason why
teachers are so universally disliked. Timothy even managed
to take felicitous advantage of a slight interruption to his
discourse : when Tom Billington arrived from his post at
the Lamb ten minutes late, and massively edged his way
to a seat, Timothy paused to let him settle, and brought
him in gracefully when he resumed : 'I was just saying,
Tom, that . . .' All in all, the assembled inhabitants of
Twytching felt that he was doing a very good piece of
public relations for them, or con job as they put it to themselves, and they glowed in the conviction that the gentlemen
from Broadwich must be getting the idea that this was
a really united and go-ahead little community.

This new fund of self-confidence and feeling that he could
bask in a general approval had only carried Timothy a
little way further in his discourse when he was thoroughly
disconcerted by the sight of the main radio chappie –
Livermore, wasn't it? – slipping out of his seat at the back
of the hall, and out through the swing doors at the back.
For a few minutes Timothy hoped it might be no more than
a call of nature, but if it was it was not of the sort that can
be relieved quickly, for Ted Livermore did not reappear.
That was a bit thick, thought Timothy, speaking of the
need for a united community effort, he shouldn't have come
at all if he was going to do that. Bloody off-putting, and
rude into the bargain. Made you wonder about the whole

idea of commercial radio when you saw the sort they were recruiting. 'Just one big push is what we need,' he said stirringly, when his mood was further depressed by the movement of an arm and the dropping of a gaze at the back of the hall. Timothy was possessed by the suspicion, which soon strengthened into a conviction, that Harold Thring had put a hand on Jack Edgar's thigh.

From this point on Timothy rather tailed off, and his introduction was brought to a much speedier conclusion than he had wished, since he found he could give little dramatic heart to his peroration. But there was no lack of speakers from the body of the hall, anxious to back him up in proving that Twytching was a lively, thrusting, go-ahead little community. Little Miss Marriot put in a say about the drama group, and blushingly confessed that they were short of young men, which won her a burst of rustic guffawing from the hall and a flutter of the eyelashes from Harold Thring. Mrs McGregor, the doctor's wife, contributed a mystic piece about the place of flowers in the life of the town, and what each and every member of the community could do about making Twytching a more spiritually satisfying place to live in by means of flower-arrangements. Mrs Brewer inevitably appealed for volunteers for meals-on-wheels, and somebody else wondered why there were no keep-fit classes.

Things rather began to degenerate after that. Someone complained about the lack of dentists in Twytching, and the length of time one had to spend waiting to see the doctor at surgery time. Someone else complained about delays in the postal service, and finally Mrs Buller, a determined little woman and a conscientious complainer and troublemaker, got up and gave it out as her impression that this town was run by a small clique, and that it was high time that a bit of democracy was introduced into the running of things around here. There was enough truth in all this for a timid little murmur of sympathy to run around the hall. Mrs Withens bridled fit to kill, and Timothy hurriedly pointed out that elections to the Council were democratically conducted, that anyone could stand, and that he was sure that any help Mrs Buller felt able to give to all the various voluntary organizations in the community would be very welcome indeed – and so on for some minutes. Not quite liking the way things were going, he pulled the meeting together by proposing a few unexceptionable resolutions, setting up a couple of working parties, and then bringing the meeting to a platitudinous close. Everyone breathed a sigh of relief that this strenuous bout of civic duty was at an end and began stirring in their seats and drawing their furs and their duffels around them. As people began filing out Timothy was quite sure he saw Harold Thring removing his hand from Jack Edgar's thigh.

Wisely as it turned out, for Harold was the inevitable centre of attention as people came to the back of the hall, and settled into little groups, either around him or watching him. He basked in the open expression of popular interest. The ladies whose cakes, wines, babies, gardens and cats he had enthused over during his last visit were assiduous in thrusting their greetings at him, so that his little wave of acknowledgement became quite limp. Jack Edgar kept him in conversation for a minute or two, calculatedly not seeming too pressing, but in any case Harold seemed to have lost interest and detached himself from him in order to swop words with Tom Billington, though whether for his own pleasure or to delay his return to the Lamb, who can say? Tom Billington responded with genial tolerance : he'd known that type in the East End. One or two of the hardier ladies gathered around them, Timothy Jimson tagged self-importantly along, and quite a nice little conversation got going.

'I will say this,' said Mrs Brewer, with the feathery hat and the vaguely fishy smell, 'I think you'll find people in Twytching will choose a very nice type of music. And it's not so easy to find these days, what with all that Radio

One stuff, and these cassock recorders that the kids have going the whole time.'

'We cater for all types at Radio Broadwich,' said Harold with his brilliant smile, shaking his orange hair-do provocatively at her.

'We're very musical in our household,' said Mrs Buller, smiling forthcomingly at her pregnant daughter in tow. 'We've got twenty-five long-players, so that will give you some idea. Everything from the very popular like the Beatles to the severely classical like the Warsaw Concerto!'

Harold stored this little gem up for telling at his next Gay Lib party, and said : 'That's what I call being catholic.'

Mrs Buller seemed about to put in a correction of her religious position, but her daughter thrust out her stomach and put in a say on her own account :

'I do think, though, you want to avoid getting stuck with the middle-aged, see what I mean? Well, you want to have some young people on, don't you, not teenagers I don't mean, 'course you wouldn't want anyone ignorant, or anything, but more of the young parent group, like, I mean otherwise it'll be the oldest inhabitant and all that stuff, see what I mean, don't you?'

'I see what you mean, ducky,' said Harold. 'You don't have to rub my nose in it.'

'No, but you can see her point in a way,' said Timothy judiciously. 'Of course you've got to have all the community leaders, and the artistic figures and so on and so forth, but then perhaps there ought to be one or two *ordinary* figures – representative citizens so to speak, part of the rising generation.'

'Perhaps we could have a raffle,' said Harold, perking up again. 'Only guaranteed ordinary citizens to buy tickets. First prize, an interview on *This is Twytching.*'

'Very Gilbert-and-Sullivan,' said Timothy, with a sycophantic little laugh.

'Of course we do see that the leaders of the town have to

be on,' said little Miss Potts loyally, 'that's only right. The world would get a very strange impression of Twytching if we didn't hear from Mrs Withens, wouldn't they?'

She looked around the group appealingly, but everyone maintained a respectful silence, especially as the lady in question was at that very moment steaming out of the hall and giving a greeting to Harold designed to express a degree of mutual understanding and agreement which did not stretch as far as actual approval of him on her part. There was a moment of uneasy silence.

'On the other hand,' said Timothy when he could be quite sure she was out of earshot, 'she can hardly be allowed to dictate who should and who should not appear.'

'Nobody's dictating to *us,* ducky,' said Harold, bristling with professional jealousy, 'I assure *you*. My Ted's got ideas of his own, and so have I, come to that.'

'That's nice to know,' said Mrs Buller with emphasis.

'Not that Deborah hasn't been an absolute *sweetie,*' Harold went on, 'and awfully co-operative and all that. Couldn't have been nicer, as I'm sure you all know.' And Harold gave an outrageous wink. Everyone relaxed a little, though poor little Miss Potts looked very bewildered.

'So nothing's really been decided yet, then?' said Mrs Buller, looking towards her Val and her Val's Sam as a couple eminently suited to represent the future of Twytching – as indeed it could be argued that they were.

'Nothing at all yet,' said Harold. 'Apart from Mrs Mailer, everything's completely open still.'

'Mrs Mailer,' came a ragged chorus, in a variety of intonations suggestive of surprise, disapproval and I-might-have-guessed.

'Yes, she's on. I don't know the lady myself, haven't had the pleasure yet. But Ted says she's on – that's our producer – lovely boy. Apart from her, all the places are vacant – just slots waiting to be filled up. But of course we've got our ideas . . .' and here Harold gazed with admiration and affection at Tom Billington, who had been standing by in a strong silent manner, rather as he did when the talk turned to politics in his bar. Jack Edgar felt distinctly put out, and wondered whether he ought to mention that he took PT classes at school.

After this the little group began to break up. Jack Edgar took himself off home, pretty sure that he was not likely to get any further with Harold Thring that night. Timothy Jimson was less wise, and tagged along with Harold and Tom Billington to the Lamb, where they found Ted Livermore drinking pints of beer with a moderately satisfied smile on his face in a snug corner of the saloon bar. All Timothy's indignation returned. Bloody cheek, he thought, coming away from the meeting just to come along here and swill beer. And he downed a quick scotch and left. The rest of the audience drifted away from the primary school hall in their various directions, some chatting and comparing notes, and wondering what that Mrs Mailer had done to get on, others singly and brooding, to pub or bed or late-night TV. After closing time a further stream dribbled their way home, and the sound of cheerios and hiccups occasionally disturbed the night air until finally peace descended and the drowsy murmurs of Twytching life stilled themselves to nothingness as the lights went off and the streets were empty. The night was cold, and the courting couples kept themselves indoors, so no home-coming lovers from the bluebell woods saw Alison Mailer, who was lying beside the path with her head bashed

CHAPTER VI

A DEATH IN THE FAMILY

Jean Jimson was half conscious for much of Tuesday morning of bustle next door, of comings and goings, and she wondered vaguely whether they had anything to do with Alison's 'business', which she was no more able to fathom the nature of than Timothy had been. But Jean was not the type to spend her life spying on her friends and acquaintances, conscious as she was that her life had conundrums enough, and she had her eldest in bed with a nasty cold and cough, so the Jimson household did not evince that twitching of the net curtain which is the invariable sign of interest and concern in an English village. She washed up, cleared up mountains of toys, and listened to *Waggoner's Walk* with her usual cheerful uncertainty as to which character was which.

At twelve o'clock, however, she found she had to go and buy a few things at the inevitable Mrs Leaze, and she pushed her youngest, a heavy, sleepy child, down the hill to the supermarket, not even noticing the unusually large numbers of gossiping pairs and groups on her way. When she got there, however, she was scarcely given time to get to the refrigerator, with its grubby packets of cheese, and to pause undecided before tasteless Cheddar and tasteless Wensleydale, before she was made aware of the fact that for once she was an extremely popular customer.

'Oh, Mrs Jimson!' said Mrs Leaze, breathless and emphatic, all straggly hair and petticoat, and waddling towards her in a perfect lather of interested friendliness. 'I've been wondering all morning if you'd come in. I never did, really, I feel so shocked, right inside me, I do, I don't know what I'm doing. And I thought if anybody knew the truth you would, and it's never 'appened before in Twytching, not to my knowledge it 'asn't, I never thought it would, but they say it 'as, and 'oo's to say 'oo to believe because people do talk something terrible and it may be a lot of smoke without fire, though they do say you can't 'ave it, but *is* it right, Mrs Jimson, *is* it? – in complete confidence of course.'

'I really don't follow you, Mrs Leaze,' said Jean, embarrassed at for some reason no longer being the passive recipient of news but the expected provider of it. She chose the Wensleydale and prepared herself for a quick dash round the other shelves and a hasty exit. 'I'm sure I haven't got any news about anything you won't have heard already. I'm home all day, you know.'

Mrs Leaze almost wailed with disappointment. 'Oh, Mrs Jimson, don't go all clammy on me! I've been waiting for you to come in and tell me for certain one way or another. I just can't stand the strain any longer, not with my 'art. And being a neighbour it stands to reason you must know.'

'I'm afraid I don't *know* at all, Mrs Leaze,' said Jean coldly. 'In fact, I haven't the faintest idea what you're talking about.'

'Well, about Mrs Mailer, of course,' said Mrs Leaze, coming unpleasantly close. 'Is it true?'

'Is what true? What's she done now?' said Jean, careful not to show any great interest.

'What's she *done*? You mean you don't *know*?' shrieked Mrs Leaze, convinced at last and preparing to switch roles to that of imparter of information instead of wriggler out. 'She's dead, that's what.'

'Dead?'

'Done in. She's been and got 'erself done in.'

'I don't believe it,' said Jean. One never does believe one's friends are dead, unless they are the dying type. 'It must be nonsense. I saw her only yesterday.'

'Did you, Mrs Jimson, *did* you?' panted Mrs Leaze.

"Ow did she look? Did she look as if she knew it was going to 'appen? Threatened, like – or 'aunted?'

'She looked just as she always does,' said Jean firmly. 'I'm sure you'll find it's just a lot of silly gossip based on nothing. Or else it's a really nasty joke. Some people round here have a very unpleasant sense of humour.'

'But it's *not*, Mrs Jimson, it's *not*. She's been found – in the bluebell woods, some say, or in that field near you with the fancy name. Nobody's quite sure, but she 'as been found. And 'er 'ead was all bashed in – an 'orrible wound it was, they say.'

Jean had to pause. She could hardly believe that Alison was dead, yet she had no hard reasons for thinking she was alive. And she remembered the bustle next door.

'Who says?' she asked.

'Mrs Brewer was full of it – she come in round about 'uppast ten, so was Miss Potts when she come in at 'er usual time, it's going all round the village. Only nobody seems to know anything for certain, 'ardly.'

'What about Cressida?' said Jean.

''Oo?' asked Mrs Leaze.

'Cressida. Mrs Mailer's daughter.'

'I don't know anything about 'er, Mrs Jimson. I don't know anything about anything.'

'I must go and see them,' said Jean, a vision of the calm, serious, pretty little girl rising before her. 'She should come in with us. She can't just be left in the house. Here, take that, Mrs Leaze. I'll come back for the change later.'

And she thrust into Mrs Leaze's hand a pound note, and began off up the hill in the direction of home, as fast as the push-chair would allow her. But not fast enough to get out of hearing of Mrs Leaze's supplicating voice, she having shuffled to the shop door in order to shrill after her:

'Be *careful*, Mrs Jimson, 'cos you never know, do you? Would you give me a tinkle when you've been there? Won't take a minute. Just so's I know you're all right.'

Jean left her youngest sleeping in his push-chair on the

front lawn. As she walked between her and Alison's so different houses a complex tangle of emotions took possession of her mind – doubt, anxiety, and a feeling of unreality. But eventually, gaining on them, came a feeling that such things did, after all, happen, that there was no reason why her life should be immune from them. And that Alison Mailer was not, in fact, an absolutely inconceivable murder victim, even though she had never considered her anything worse than aggravating and foolish. Her disbelief flooded away from her when she saw a policeman standing at the front door.

She unlatched the wrought-iron gate and walked a little unsteadily up the drive. She took in the brilliantly even and weed-free front lawn and the decorously blooming flower beds. A sense overwhelmed her of the triviality of Alison's life, the pettinesses on which it had been frittered away, so that now she seemed no longer even aggravating, merely pathetic. It seemed to her that she had bartered her reality for a colour television and a leather Scandinavian lounge suite. When she got up to the front door she found her eyes inexplicably filling with tears, and she had to brush them away. The constable on the door, sturdy and running to fat, was Fred Lockett, the oldest of the town's policemen. Jean knew his wife.

'Hello, Fred,' she said.

'I'm afraid you can't go in, Mrs Jimson,' said Fred Lockett. 'I've got very strict instructions.'

'I don't want to,' said Jean. 'Does this mean it's true?'

Fred reacted slowly. He was not used to this kind of thing, and though Inspector Parrish had impressed upon him slowly and clearly what he was and was not to do, he was better at doing what he had always done before than he was at doing what he was told. He had to put his head on one side and think for a bit.

'I don't know as I can say anything about that, Mrs Jimson. In any case, I don't know what folks are saying.'

Jean decided not to circle round the subject. She didn't

want Constable Lockett to think of her as one of the Twytching Gossip Ring, on the ferret for information.

'I'm worried about Cressida,' she said. 'The little girl. Is her father here now, or not? She shouldn't be alone in the house, and perhaps it would be best to get her out of it, anyway. I thought I could take her in with me.'

This Constable Lockett understood at once. He was a kindly man, and none of Inspector Parrish's instructions could override his concern for the wide-eyed creature who was somewhere inside. He had heard no crying, but he had been standing there trying to imagine what it must be like for her.

'Now that would be kind,' he said. 'She's all alone there, you see, because they haven't made contact with the father yet. They think he went by train to London today as usual – Tuesday is his day, you know. Would you like to slip in and get her now? She was in the living-room when the inspector left.'

Jean went into the hall, feeling a mixture of guilt and dread. She shouldn't be here, she didn't want to be here, yet she was here. She felt almost like an accomplice of Mrs Leaze. How difficult it was to get one's thoughts in order when someone you disliked had died. It was still more difficult, somehow, when you were in her house. The big hall, with everything neatly shut away in cupboards, with no signs of the humans who had come in and out, and the arty wallpaper at the far end which somehow gave you the idea you were losing your balance. The house was like Alison herself : it made you feel at less than your best. Jean paused at the doorway to the sitting-room.

Cressida Mailer was sitting at the table, writing. As always there was a quiet, self-contained air about her, and Jean was struck with it more than ever at such a time. She looked up as Jean came into the room. Her eyes were slightly red, but there was no sign of exaggerated grief. This gave Jean an odd feeling that she was exaggerating the matter, or that nothing had really happened in spite of Constable Lockett's presence outside. Cressida's eyes were dark, deep, hooded by self-concealment, which perhaps had become habitual with her. She was twelve.

'Hello, Mrs Jimson,' she said, with something of her mother's composure. 'It was nice of you to come.'

'Are you all right, Cressida?' asked Jean, not quite knowing what to say at such a time. 'I've come to take you next door. It's wrong for you to be here alone.'

Cressida smiled a sad little smile. 'I'm quite all right, thank you, Mrs Jimson,' she said, her eyes filling with tears. 'It's nice of you to invite me, but I won't come round. Daddy should be home any time now. They're fetching him from London, and he'll expect me to be here.'

'I'm quite sure he won't expect you to be here, Cressida, or want you to be,' said Jean briskly. 'He would be far happier if you were round with us being looked after.'

'He'll want me here when he comes back,' repeated Cressida with a trace of obstinacy, 'and really I don't need looking after. But it's awfully kind of you.'

She looked down at her writing, unconsciously seeming to say, 'If there's nothing else, would you please go and let me get on with what I was doing.' Jean felt almost nonplussed, as she had always been after some of Alison's more outrageous remarks that she could not think of an immediate answer to. She had a sudden feeling that the child, never having aroused maternal instincts in Alison, inevitably suppressed any such feelings in other women whenever there was danger of their being aroused. But she had to try again.

'Cressida, you do understand that Mummy is dead, don't you?' she said, coming closer.

'Yes, Mother's dead,' said Cressida. 'The policeman told me. It's terrible. I've got to think of Daddy first of all now.'

'That's all very well, but you must see that it's wrong for you to be here on your own. Your father will be very upset, and will have to talk to the police. It wouldn't be right for you to be around while all that's going on.'

'Why?' said Cressida, and paused a second before continuing. 'I know Daddy will want me here. I shan't come, Mrs Jimson. But thank you very much for asking me.'

It was the blankest of dismissals. Jean muttered something about Cressida knowing she could always come round if she needed help, and Cressida nodded – smiling seriously, but obviously wanting to get rid of her. Jean retreated, puzzled and dissatisfied with herself, to Constable Lockett, whose bulk was still blocking the front door.

'She won't come,' she said. 'I wish she would – it seems so ghastly her being alone in the house like this, with all Alison's things around her and so on. But I don't think she's been crying too much.'

'Poor little thing, she must be weeping inside, though,' said Constable Lockett, whose mental horizon could not be widened to include a little girl who felt no grief for a dead mother. 'I know the inspector would like her out, and that's a fact. I'll tell him when he comes that you're willing to have her.'

'Thanks,' said Jean. 'I'll be in all day.' And she was about to take her leave when she saw a police car draw up in the street outside and Arnold Mailer get out.

His face was grey-white, like grimy plaster, and his mouth was slack, as if he had lost control of his face muscles. The slackness seemed to have affected his whole body, and he looked fifteen years older than when Jean saw him last. For a moment as he got out of the car it seemed as if he did not know where he was. Inspector Parrish came round the car, a worried, sympathetic look on his face, and jogged his arm to start him up the pathway. Then Arnold seemed to collect his thoughts, as if he really was taking in the news for the first time, and with a giant effort he co-ordinated himself and hurried towards the house.

As he passed Jean he seemed dimly to register who she was, and muttered, 'Must see Cressida. Damned shame I wasn't here when she heard,' and pushed his way through the front door. Jean had time to catch a glimpse of haggard, haunted eyes, and hair that seemed to have been torn into by frantic hands, hair that seemed to have greyed overnight. Then he was gone.

Jean looked up at Inspector Parrish, who had followed Mailer more slowly up the garden path.

'I tried to get the little girl away,' she said, conscious of some absurdity in the description, 'but she wouldn't come. She simply refused.'

'Pity,' said Parrish, with his air of country consideration. 'But we can't force her. That might be worst of all.' He turned to Constable Lockett. 'I'm going to be unprofessional – I'll give them half an hour together. They'll need it. I shan't get any sense out of him till he's sure she's all right. Keep an eye on them as far as you can while I'm gone.'

He and Jean turned to go down the drive. Through the window of the sitting-room Jean had a brief picture of Arnold and Cressida. They were both on their feet, he suddenly seeming immensely tall as he stroked her hair and bent to kiss her. Cressida had buried her head in his chest. Jean wondered whether her eyes were still dry, and hoped not. She turned away, almost ashamed, as if she had been caught watching an indecent act. Displays of emotion were rare in Timothy Jimson's house.

'You should have got her in here,' said Timothy later in the day. 'It would have been interesting to see how she was reacting.'

Jean could hardly believe her ears. She looked hard at Timothy to see if he meant to be as heartless as he sounded. He bridled visibly and put on a front of pomposity.

'To me. As a writer,' he said.

CHAPTER VII

CONSTABULARY DUTIES

When the police photographers had taken the body (lying in an unaccustomedly inelegant posture) from every possible angle, and then taken two or three more for luck, and when the pathologist had done his work, the ambulance men, supervised by the police surgeon, gingerly lifted the body on to a stretcher, and drove off with it to the morgue at Barstowe. Something of its usual rural quietness returned to the scene, though it was a quietness only maintained by dint of a police guard stationed a hundred yards or so away from the body's position in both directions along the lane to the bluebell wood. Inspector Parrish, his friendly, comfortable body having taken on something of a new purpose and firmness already, still stood way back from where the body had lain, looking at the ground and pondering. Inspector Parrish had a highly rural ponder, and none of his inferiors interrupted one lightly. Sergeant Feather and Sergeant Underwood stood by watching him and waiting, the latter now and then patting down her skirt a little nervously. She had never before been on a murder case, and – Twytching being what it was – this one could be a once-in-a-lifetime experience. She didn't want to disgrace herself by some foolishness of word or deed, and since the men at the station mainly kept her on cases of lollipops purloined in the school playground and pets who had absconded from old-age pensioners, it wasn't easy to decide how to behave. She had already concluded that her best cue for the moment was silence, and she was right. Eventually Inspector Parrish raised his head and spoke.

'Can't see that the ground around tells us much,' he said. 'Too dry, that's the trouble.'

'No signs of dragging, though,' said Sergeant Feather. 'There would be if she had been, dry as it is.'

'True,' said Parrish. 'True enough. But where does that get us?'

'Well, I suppose you could say it tells us that if a woman did it, she probably did it right here. I'm pretty sure a woman couldn't have carried her here.'

'*Most* women couldn't,' said Parrish cautiously, and wondered why a mental picture of Mrs Withens rose to his mind. 'But why in God's name should she be carried here at all? It's not as though the body was hidden – it was right by the side of the path. Just waiting to be found.'

'She was only wearing a cardigan,' said Sergeant Underwood tentatively. 'It was quite a thick one – natural wool, I think, and very smart. But still, it doesn't seem very much to have on for a cold night like last night.'

Inspector Parrish considered for a moment, but finally he shook his head. 'Maybe,' he said. 'But that sort of woman thinks about effect first of all. Think how some women waltz around a freezing ballroom with all their arms and shoulders and what-have-you bare as the day they were born. Daft I call it – but you wouldn't even guess they were slightly chilly from the look of them. Mrs Mailer was very much that type, so far as I knew the lady. If she thought she looked good in her cardigan, she'd wear it, willy-nilly.'

'Do you think she was meeting a man, then?' asked Stephen Feather, who always spoke to Parrish as to a father, though slightly more respectfully.

'Now how should I know, lad?' said Parrish impatiently. 'We haven't the first idea as to why she was here, if she was here, or who she was meeting if she was meeting anyone. In any case, I'd say she was the sort who was just as likely to dress up to meet another woman as to meet a man, wouldn't you, Betty?'

'More,' said Sergeant Underwood briefly.

'Certainly she looked smartly turned out to my unpractised eye,' said Parrish. 'Isn't that so, Betty?'

Sergeant Underwood nodded. 'Really well-cut skirt, very smart blouse – Harrods, or that type of shop. Good things, and fresh on – clean apart from the dust and so on.'

She shuddered briefly, as she remembered looking closely at the collar and shoulders of the blouse.

'That's what I thought,' said Parrish. 'Then again, what does it tell you? I never saw Mrs Mailer looking any other way. There's some women always look like a Daimler ad even in their own homes, so I'm told. Even put on special make-up to go to bed at nights – isn't that so, Stephen?'

'I wouldn't know, sir,' said Sergeant Feather, rather stiffly. He was a rather stiff young man.

'Out of your class, eh?' said Inspector Parrish, wheezing happily to himself. 'I suppose so, on your salary. Anyway, the poor creature looked good to the end, which I imagine would have pleased her. Rather a funny position she'd got herself into, but otherwise a credit to the town. Apart from the back of her head.' He walked gingerly to where Bert Carrington, on his way that morning to play truant in the bluebell woods, had found Alison lying face down in the dust and dirt, with the very nasty wound in the back of her head. Parrish's sharp eyes darted around and about the spot for the twentieth time, but they lighted on nothing. 'Almost too orderly somehow,' he said.

At that moment the constable in the police car parked fifty yards away, where the track became too narrow to drive over, signalled to Parrish, and he plop-plopped over, puffing and wiping his forehead. Two minutes later he was back.

'That was Barstowe. The husband's been contacted. He'll be there on the down train in three quarters of an hour. They contacted him at Audley End, and he changed trains, I guess. Nasty news to be given on a railway station. I'd better go and meet him I suppose.'

'Odd,' said Sergeant Feather. 'Why hadn't he reported the disappearance earlier? Doc said he thought she'd been dead nigh on twelve hours or more. You wouldn't just blithely get on the train and go to London if your wife hadn't shown up all night.'

'Some wives don't get their husband's breakfast,' said Inspector Parrish. 'And as you'd know if you had the sense to become a married man – plenty don't sleep in the same room as their husbands.'

'Some advertisement for marriage,' said Sergeant Feather. 'Still, I'm impressed by your knowledge of this woman's sleeping habits – sleeps alone, wears make-up in bed. First the consequence of the second, perhaps. Anything else you know you haven't passed on yet?'

Stephen Feather sometimes became unusually sharp when the subject of marriage came up. He resented Parrish's rather obvious attempts to push him into the arms of Sergeant Underwood.

'I want the whole area round here searched,' said Parrish, ignoring him. 'With a toothcomb – or a bloody fine rake, anyway. I'll get you reinforcements from Chetley and Highton and round about if I can. Meanwhile no one's allowed anywhere near here – keep the blighters where they are now.'

And he waved his hand to the spot some way off along the path into Twytching proper, where a couple of constables were keeping under their beady eyes a scared but delighted little band of Twytchingites, who were watching the every movement of all the policemen on the scene, some using field-glasses and all with expressions on their faces that suggested they were congratulating themselves on performing their public duty. They would have worn the same expression if they had been watching a pageant of Twytching history, or if they had gone along to see Miss Potts perform a ritual burning of obscene books in the High Street.

'Have fun,' said Parrish, 'whatever you do,' and he lumbered off towards the police car.

This was not the last they saw of him that morning,

though. A little over an hour later, when Sergeant Feather's stomach clock was telling him it was his lunch-time or close on, he lumbered back.

'Found anything?' Parrish asked Feather, who had been bent over or actually on his hands and knees most of the time since he left, and hardly felt in the best of moods.

'A tin of boot-polish, three Coca-Cola bottles, twenty-four empty cigarette packets, and last Thursday's *Daily Mirror*,' said Stephen Feather, 'and various things I wouldn't mention to your chaste ears.'

'Splendid work,' said Parrish. 'Keep at it. I'm sure they all fit in somewhere – help to make the pattern clear. It's all a matter of finding the right pattern, you know. Eliminate the improbable, and what you have left is the bloody impossible. Don't miss an inch of ground. I'm off to have a cuppa at the station.'

'What did you do with Mailer, then?' asked Feather.

'Left him at home,' said Parrish comfortably. 'Poor chappie's just lost his wife. If he did it, we'll get him, sure as eggs. If he didn't, he'll need time to recover from the shock, talk to that daughter of his, and so on. It's not for an old bachelor like me to intrude on him. I'll just drink a leisurely cuppa and then go round to him in an hour or so.'

'Don't keep mentioning tea,' said Stephen, bending back to his task. 'It's all right for some.'

'I'd have sent some out for you, but I doubt I can spare the men,' said Parrish. 'Still, you'll be through in a couple of hours or so, won't you? Taste even better by then.'

And he lumbered off again, shaking with benevolent laughter. Sergeant Feather sometimes thought he was making his life on duty so uncomfortable in order to make the thought of marriage and a home more attractive. Why doesn't he mind his own damned business? said Feather to himself, digging up a dead match embedded in the soil. He suspected Parrish already had plans for him and Sergeant Underwood to walk out of the local church through an archway of raised truncheons. Very romantic, no doubt, and a suitably ludicrous ending to a marriage conducted by the present vicar of Twytching. But Stephen Feather did not intend to be married off by anyone, least of all by his bachelor boss. Stephen Feather did not, for the moment, intend to be married at all. And meanwhile there were another two hours or more of Coca-Cola bottles, empty match-boxes and contraceptives. And Inspector Parrish, meanwhile, was no doubt sitting in the station, feet up, drinking his tea. Roll on promotion.

Arnold Mailer was a tall man, and he and Inspector Parrish seemed comfortably to fill the tiny study – the smallest bedroom upstairs, in fact – which was where they talked later in the day. Mailer had asked him to sit down in the lounge, and had seemed to assume that Cressida, wide-eyed yet still sadly calm, would be allowed to sit in on the interview. Inspector Parrish found this oddly innocent – as if, because he knew he had nothing unpleasant to reveal, the Inspector would have nothing unpleasant to ask. But he had insisted on finding somewhere else to talk.

Mailer had got a better grip on himself in the hour he had been given with his daughter, though his eyes sometimes contracted from the immediate scene, as if in a sort of disbelief at what had happened, or a wondering grief. When he put a cigarette in his mouth (a cheap brand, Parrish noted, a type often smoked by men with wives like Alison Mailer) his hand shook as he tried to manipulate the lighter. But the first inhalation seemed to calm him again, and he sat back in his desk chair – Parrish had a very old armchair, obviously inherited or bought at a junk sale for the room in the house that didn't matter because it wasn't seen – and waited for the first question.

'When did you last see your wife, Mr Mailer?'

Parrish felt vaguely Cromwellian in putting the question. A spasm passed over Mailer's face – rather a good-looking face, Parrish decided, for a man of fifty or so, and probably positively handsome twenty years ago.

'Yesterday. Yesterday at dinner-time.'

'What time would that be?'

'Well – I got in from work about six, and we had sherry. I suppose we must have eaten about a quarter to seven.'

'All three of you?'

'That's right.'

'Do you know what your wife had been doing during the day?'

'Doing? No, we didn't talk about that.'

'What did you talk about?'

'Oh, the usual things. Let's see. Prices in the shops, the radio team being here, redecorating the lounge . . . That's all I remember.'

'And then you had dinner. I suppose your wife must have spent some part of the day cooking.'

'I imagine so – she and Cressy.'

'And after the meal, what did you do?'

'Well, I had one or two papers to put in order – up here, you know. Then I went to the meeting at the village school.'

'Oh yes, the Amenities Protection Group – Mr Jimson's affair, isn't it? Was your wife with you?'

'No, I went on my own.'

'You're . . . er . . . interested in environmental matters and that sort of thing, are you, sir?' asked Parrish rather tentatively.

'Well yes, within reason. But that wasn't why I went. Alison – that's my wife – was on the committee, but she wasn't going, and I thought I ought to show the flag.'

'I see, sir.'

'I wished I hadn't later on, in a way. I got the impression it was a sort of put-up job, for the benefit of the Radio Broadwich production team. I'm a bit out of village life, and I hadn't realized.'

'Did your wife give any reason for not going – any other appointment, for example?'

'No, she didn't say. I think she just said she was bored

with it. She got bored very easily, I'm afraid. Perhaps I shouldn't have brought her to a little town like this. She liked it at first, but really it wasn't her sort of life.'

And Arnold Mailer jerkily grabbed a handkerchief from his pocket and shamefacedly wiped his eyes.

'So your wife stayed at home. And you have no reason to think she might have been intending to meet anyone later? I'd better be specific : that she might have had an appointment with a man, for example?'

Nothing could be more genuine than Arnold Mailer's wide-eyed surprise as he met Inspector Parrish's gaze.

'That's just not on, Inspector, no question of it at all. My God, I suppose that's what these village tabbies are likely to be saying, isn't it?'

'Very probably, sir. But it's a question I had to ask as well.'

'It's not on the cards at all, Inspector. Alison wasn't that sort of person at all.'

'So your wife, as far as you know, was intending to stay at home. But you didn't see her when you got back from the meeting?'

'No. I assumed she'd gone to bed.'

'And had she? Had the bed been slept in?'

'I haven't . . . been in there. Cressy says not.'

Inspector Parrish shifted his cosy weight in bachelor embarrassment in his armchair.

'You don't . . . use the same room at night, sir?'

'That's right. I have to get up early, especially on the days I go to London. My wife is a late riser as a rule. She didn't like to be disturbed, you see.'

'And she was usually early to bed, was she, sir? You say you assumed she had gone to bed when you came back from the meeting.'

'That depended, Inspector. Sometimes she was up till all hours. She went out fairly often, had a lot of friends and so on. But sometimes she went to bed not long after dinner. As I say, she bored easily.'

'So when you got back from the meeting – about ten that would be, wouldn't it? – you didn't look in on her?'

'No. I had a scotch, read a little, and went to bed.'

'What were you reading, if you don't mind my asking?'

'Solzhenitsyn. My wife had told – had asked me to read it and tell her what it was about.'

'And this morning, then, you didn't look into her room before you left for work?'

'No, she wouldn't have thanked me for that. Except of course that she wasn't there . . .' He paused, and slumped a little forward in his chair, thinking. 'Wasn't there . . .'

Inspector Parrish cut in quickly. 'Then today was one of the days you went to London, was it, sir?'

'That's right. Tuesdays and Fridays.'

'And you made your own breakfast in the morning?'

'Yes. Or Cressy sometimes helps me, and has hers as well. She likes getting up early.'

She likes having breakfast alone with you, Inspector Parrish thought. There was no disguising the affection between father and daughter.

'What is your business, sir?' he asked.

'Construction firm, with a bit of property dealing thrown in,' said Arnold Mailer. 'We operate mainly in East Anglia, but we have London interests, and there's usually enough Stock Exchange business to keep me busy on those two days. I'm in charge of the financial side of things.'

'Is business thriving?' asked Parrish banally, not necessarily expecting an honest answer.

'Is any business these days?' answered Arnold. 'But we've done well in the past, and that should carry us over the lean times. Of course anyone who has to do with property has a bad reputation these days – people say we're all sharks. But our firm has made a good name for itself – in pretty murky waters, I admit – and that means a lot when money's short, as now. People are only willing these days to deal with the sort of firm they know they can trust.'

'Well, I think that's about all, for the moment anyway,

sir,' said Parrish. 'I'll probably have to be troubling you again about details before very long. I suppose you'd rather I didn't talk to your daughter today, wouldn't you? I can hold it over for twenty-four hours easily enough.'

'I'd be grateful if you would,' said Arnold. 'She's very upset, though she doesn't show things as much as other kids – terribly self-contained, and always has been. If you could hold off for a bit I'd take it very kindly, though I'm sure she won't have anything she can add.'

'Children sometimes see a lot,' said Parrish, adding to himself that they habitually saw more than the besotted kind of husband. 'I'll be back tomorrow, sir,' he said aloud, 'and I'll probably have more questions for you too, I'm afraid, sir. After that I suppose you'd prefer to send the young lass away for a bit – to relatives or something.'

Arnold Mailer looked at him naïvely, as if the thought simply hadn't occurred to him before.

'Do you think so, Inspector? I hadn't thought of it. Surely she'd be better with me than with strangers?'

'I just thought the house . . . and having the police here, and people talking, and so on. And the funeral eventually.'

'She's a child with a lot of imagination,' said Arnold Mailer. 'I think she'd worry a lot more about those things if she wasn't around to see them. And frankly, I don't think she'd go.'

'Well, that's up to you, sir,' said Parrish. 'But I'm afraid I'll have to have my men give this house a thorough going-over – in fact they'd better start as soon as it's convenient to you.'

'As soon as you like, of course, Inspector. Though I can't think what you can expect to find.'

'I don't, sir – so far I have no ideas, no theories, nothing. That's why we have to start from scratch and look up all sorts of avenues. Well, thank you anyway, sir. My men will be round in a half-hour or so, and I'll make sure they give you as little trouble as possible.'

And Inspector Parrish let himself out of the study and

went down the stairs, looking into the lounge, where
Cressida was still sitting at the table over an exercise book,
and didn't look up as he passed. The contrast between
the trendy but rather boring hall and the man he had just
been talking to struck him. He wondered why he had liked
Arnold Mailer as a man, and thought it must be partly
his unlikeness to his own house. He was a living contrast
to all around him, but he lacked the elementary self-con-
sciousness that would have told him so. It might be that
to have lived happily with a woman such as Alison Mailer
argued a fairly high degree of stupidity as far as some areas
of life were concerned, but these were, after all, areas in
which a great many men were fortunate enough to be
dense. For the thousandth time Inspector Parrish regretted
his bachelor status, and thought he would have liked to
have a chance to cultivate a similar denseness. For the
thousandth time he wondered how sincere he was in re-
gretting his bachelorhood. It was an exercise in self-analysis
unusual in a common-sensical sort of man, and one that
gave him endless food for thought.

Swapping a few words and admonitions with Constable
Lockett on the door, Parrish went out into the open air.

The biggest room in the Twytching Police Station, apart
from that in which the general public was received, was
officially Inspector Parrish's, though Sergeant Feather also
had a desk in the corner, where he typed in an enthusiastic
and imprecise manner when the occasion demanded. His
precision was not helped by continual fencing matches with
his superior over why he didn't get married to Sergeant
Underwood, and a further range of topics – personal, social
and political. Sergeant Feather diverted Inspector Parrish's
bachelor enthusiasm for marrying off his younger acquaintances into a number of channels, and this little back room
was one of the few places where the Great Debate on the
Common Market had actually got going. It was a scruffy,
slightly dirty room, but Inspector Parrish had tried to make

it reasonably homely by bringing in a few sticks of furniture he had inherited from a dead sister, and sticking up on the wall colour photographs cut from calendars. He encouraged pictures of the Sussex Downs and the Lake District, and felt that Norway and the Swiss Alps were slightly on the sensational side.

Later on the same Tuesday Inspector Parrish tried to explain to Sergeant Feather the effect Arnold Mailer had made on him – not making too good a job of it either, for though he was far more loquacious with his sergeant than with any other living soul, he basically mistrusted words.

'Put it this way,' he said. 'If I was buying a property, or doing a deal, I'd trust him. Nothing showy, nothing put on. Just a straightforward kind of chap – very quiet, very controlled.'

'Still waters run deep,' said Sergeant Feather, leafing through his report on the finding of the body.

'Still waters run deep, my fat aunt,' said Parrish, irritated as usual by his sergeant's preference for cliché over hard thinking. 'I've known still waters about as deep as a bath in war-time. Still, in this case there's a lot of strong feeling – you're right that far. Quite broke down when he heard the news, so I heard from the Barstowe people. Pulled himself together well later on, though – perfectly clear when I spoke to him. Did you ever come across him at all?'

'Just once, in the High Street, about a couple of months ago, I guess. Had his car parked a bit close to the corner. Very nice and apologetic about it. Pretty calm, easy-going sort of chap, I agree.'

'I spoke to him in the Lamb a week or so ago,' went on Parrish, 'or rather we were both there and I heard him talking to Tom behind the bar, and to Fred Brewer and that Mr Jimson. Now, I've had the idea that a lot of people in this town have been a bit jumpy over the past weeks. Just an impression of mine – a sharp word here and there, the odd look – you know what I mean. It's no more than an impression. But I didn't notice anything of the sort about Arnold Mailer.'

Sergeant Feather looked hard at his boss. He never discounted his hunches, because he saw those eyes registering, those ears almost twitching as they noticed the nuances in the most casual conversation, nuances which Parrish would never be able to explicate in words.

'What did you think was up?' asked Sergeant Feather at last.

'Haven't the foggiest,' said Parrish grumpily. 'But this damnfool radio documentary business is the obvious thing, isn't it? I imagine towns get like this whenever there's a royal visit – everyone pushing themselves forward to shake the royal paw. Same sort of thing this, in a way – same sort of opportunity to make an ass of yourself in a very public way.'

'You could be right,' said Feather. 'Or there could be something else as well, connected, you know. In a place like this everything gets all caught up with everything else. I mean, like you can still trace the after-effects of quarrels and upsets from years back if you try. And the infighting can get pretty fierce.'

'Exactly what I tried to tell Mrs Withens,' said Parrish, 'only the daft old body wouldn't listen. You know how some of these local big-wigs get such an inflated idea of –'

But he was interrupted in mid-les-majesty by the door of his office being flung open, and the gangling figure of the vicar appearing in the entrance, with the apologetic face of Sergeant Underwood visible somewhere among the ill-co-ordinated limbs, obviously wanting to explain that she'd tried to stop him but hadn't been able to. The vicar jumbled himself into the room, pointedly shut the door on Sergeant Underwood, and came forward to confront Inspector Parrish.

The Reverend Garston Tamville-Bence had come to Twytching something over five and forty years before, at about the time when the roaring twenties were subsiding into the hungry thirties, both eras making about the same impression on the sluggish current of Twytching life. At the time of his arrival he had an energetic little wife, rather pretty than otherwise, and before very long two or three children. He was not a very dynamic vicar – thank goodness, everybody said, because the last thing one wanted in Twytching was one of this new breed of clergymen with social consciences paraded for everybody's admiration. His manner and accent went down well too, being undoubtedly aristocratic: his speech – jerky, spluttery and almost impossible to understand at moments of stress – lent a particular lustre to his early sermons. After a time people began to take these things for granted, and in fact got thoroughly used to him, which was just as well, for though his wife and children disappeared with a travelling encyclopedia salesman shortly before war broke out, the vicar remained, and had, with the years, mellowed into eccentricity, and then into . . . well, into madness some people said. But most were too respectful to put a name to it, and tipped their hats to him, as in the old days, and stayed away from his church, as in the old days. With a dwindling flock, he occasionally practised exorcism, talking in tongues, and impromptu seances. Luckily none of his superiors in the Anglican Church noticed, or, if they noticed, thought it mattered, and everyone except Mrs Withens was pleased about that. Twytching did not go along with the national craze of change for change's sake.

'This business, Inspector,' chortled the vicar, spraying Parrish's desk and fixing his eye on some point in the ceiling. 'This business, now. God's hand is in it somewhere. Yes, it's there somewhere, you know. If we could but discern it.'

'I'm glad to hear it, Vicar,' said Parrish equably. 'Very glad indeed.'

'Evil is stalking the village, Inspector. Stalking! I said so last night. Publicly. But let Satan beware! God's hand is waiting, upraised, ready to strike!'

'I've no doubt you're right, Vicar,' said Parrish, 'and

it's very comforting to know.'

'Or perhaps it has struck! Eh? EH? Perhaps it has even now – yea, while we slept – struck!'

'Well, sir, evil is our business in a manner of speaking, and we're certainly doing our best to get to the bottom of this whole thing. And since we are rather – '

'Wrong, Inspector, wrong! Evil is *my* business. Crime is *your* business, but evil is *my* business. And my Lord's!'

'Well, yes, Vicar, but – '

'Murder is yours, but what goes before murder perhaps . . .' The Reverend Tamville-Bence was forced to pause in mid-sentence by a load of spittle which he could only get rid of by swallowing.

'Such as?' prompted Parrish.

'Back-biting, slandering, love of position and pomp and power, and the glories of this world . . .'

'Yes, well – '

'Letter-writing.'

'Letter-writing?' said Parrish, interested at last.

'The distribution of vile slanders through the postal service of our Earthly Lady the Queen, the committing to paper of lies and filth, of lewdness and harlotries . . .'

'And such letters – ?'

'Have been sent,' said the Reverend Tamville-Bence, jerking his face down from contemplation of the dirty ceiling and looking Parrish straight in the face, as if to make sure he was being taken seriously. 'Stamped and addressed. Sealed and delivered.' He lowered his voice mysteriously. 'Herein lies the evil that has stalked the land. Herein can be discerned the mark of the eternal enemy of mankind. And whereto shall we look for vengeance?'

'Well, the police force, sir – '

'Whereto but the Lord?' shrilled the vicar triumphantly. 'Whereto, my brethren in uniform, but the Lord?'

'Have you yourself, sir – ' began Parrish.

'For vengeance is mine, saith the Lord,' went on the vicar, retreating hurriedly from Parrish's question in the direction of the door. 'And I will repay. Note that : I WILL repay. And who knows, brothers in the law, if he hath not repaid?'

And giving a public-school cackle, like a cockerel trying to laugh, the vicar trundled himself through the door and threw himself down the passage in a thunder of overturned furniture.

'Oh my God,' said Sergeant Feather.

'No, just the vicar,' said Parrish. 'But he does have the gift of pulling you up short, I'll give him that.'

CHAPTER VIII

MATTER FOR A MAY MORNING

Alison Mailer's death did not make the front pages of the newspapers. Even the *Sun* only managed to squeeze it in on page three, and then it only gave four lines. Too many other things had happened : Mr Benn had said something nice about the British worker, and all the editors were outraged; a new mountain had been discovered somewhere in the Common Market; aspersions had been cast on the sexual purity of Miss World. Alison was relegated to the inside pages if notice was taken of her at all, and the case showed no signs of becoming a *cause célèbre*, which was the only thing that could have compensated Alison for that nasty dent in the back of her skull.

So that, though it got to Ted Livermore's ears that the delicious topic of murder was exciting the community which he was supposed to be investigating in depth for its transatlantic twin, nobody mentioned to him over Tuesday the identity of the victim. Nor did he go out of his way to discuss the matter with anyone : murders did not fit in with the totally cosy image of Twytching which he thought it his duty (for commercial reasons) to put over in his pro-

gramme. Twytching's American cousins would expec
it to be quaint, friendly, and impregnated with history and
folk-culture, and that's how it was going to be. So when
nobody brought the matter up, he didn't think it was the
sort of subject he ought to refer to himself. After a hard
day chatting to the locals, meeting up with the variou
notables whom people mentioned and trying to select the
most suitably commonplace, Ted spent the early part o
the evening in the deserted snug bar of the Lamb, where
he had a few words with Joy, including an ambiguousl
worded invitation to his room. He had spent the later par
of the evening upstairs, reading, waiting, and hoping. So
by Wednesday lunch-time he was still unaware that he had
been largely displaced as prime object of interest to the
natives of Twytching.

'Not many in this morning,' he said to Tom Billington
as he sat on the bar stool in the saloon bar, and wondered
when Joy would descend from the landlord's flat in the
upper regions (three doors along from his) and take over
the pumps.

'It'll be filling up before long,' said Tom.

'Because I'm here, you mean,' said Ted. In point of fact
Tom had meant that people would be coming in order
to use the Lamb as a discussion forum for all their variou
theories of the murder, which by two o'clock would be
solved in everybody's minds – differently in each case, but
to the satisfaction of each individual solver. But Ted's mis
take was entirely without conceit, which was far from
being one of his sins : he had been in radio and televisior
long enough now to accept unconcernedly the fact tha
he was inevitably the centre of interest in the communitie
he visited, and couldn't imagine any other state of affair
– just as Royalty patronizing the Rangers-Celtic match
probably assume that everyone has come to see them.

'Odd little place this,' said Ted.

Tom wiped away at a beer glass before replying. He wa

as unlikely to rush into things as any genuine native-born countryman.

'Nice enough little place,' he said finally. 'Sort of place we've been looking for for a long time.'

When Tom said this, Ted knew he had come to Twytching in order to go to seed. Ted devoutly hoped this process included neglecting his wife.

'Oh, it's a nice enough little place,' said Ted. 'Don't get me wrong. But the people puzzle me, you know. Of course they're all hell bent on getting on the programme – '

'Natural,' said Tom Billington.

'Oh yes, absolutely to be expected. And we know how to deal with the pushing type in our trade. On the other hand, there's something odd here : when I hint to someone they might be on, they're pleased in a way – but I get a funny feeling they're almost *afraid*. Don't quite know how to describe it.'

'Natural enough, though,' said Tom, considering. 'That too.'

'But they're not *nervous*, that's not what I mean. They're more *scared*. A look comes into their eyes – that's what I haven't seen before anywhere.'

'Wouldn't know about that,' said Tom. Was it Ted Livermore's imagination, or did a veil slide down over his eyes too – a gesture of withdrawal from that topic of conversation? At that moment Joy Billington came down, and the thought went out of Ted's mind, as did almost all other thoughts. As Tom drifted weightily away in the direction of the public bar, Ted subtly changed his personality from being chaps together with Tom to being the irresistible cosmopolitan sophisticate with the delectable Joy. Pop singers and prime ministers ask my advice, his manner said, and even the Archbishop of Canterbury is not above consulting me about his public image. Within a few minutes the innuendos and veiled invitations were falling thick and fast (for she had *not* come last night, in spite of his expectation), but before long the bar started filling up, and he had to refine his technique of seduction to a level of indirection well above the comprehension of the cheerful, direct Joy Billington.

Mrs Leaze shuffled in for her morning gin and it, her expensive fur coat just that mite too short to hide her petticoat, which had hardly known an upward turn since the murder news broke; she was joined by Mrs Buller and Val, and they sat at a corner table exchanging inaccurate information with great goodwill. Mrs Buller's Val's Sam was down the other end of the bar with Brewer the fish-monger, a jolly, smelly presence, and Dr McGregor stood near, sipping a very large neat scotch (he had asked for a simple whisky and soda, loudly, but this was a little fiction for public consumption which had been arranged with Tom Billington as soon as he arrived, and had been one of Tom's first experiences of the deceptions of simple village life). McGregor chatted to Tom about his back, as if this was the only reason he had come in. But around half past twelve the conviviality of the scene was broken for Ted by the entrance of Harold Thring.

'Ted,' Harold called urgently from the door, 'Ted!' If the name Ted could have been hissed, Harold would have hissed it.

'Hello, Harold,' said Ted, with the tolerance born of long acquaintance and a nice nature. 'Have a drink.'

Harold sidled in, throwing stiletto-sharp glances to all sides.

'Well, yes, just while I tell you. Gin and tonic, please.' He slipped his green-linen-covered bottom suggestively on to a bar stool and leaned towards Ted, who leaned back-wards.

'Have you *heard*?' asked Harold urgently.

'Heard what?' said Ted. 'About the murder?'

Harold looked terribly disappointed. 'Oh, you have. I thought you couldn't have done – sitting here as calm as you please. The point is, where does it leave us?'

'Us?' said Ted. 'Well, nowhere. We shall ignore it, of course. You couldn't mention that sort of thing on the programme, not at all the sort of thing the Yanks are after.'

'Well obviously, ducky,' said Harold crossly. 'Do you think I'm out of my mind? What I mean is: what will the big boys at Broadwich say? If they get to know we're involved?'

'Involved? Why are we involved?'

'You mean you don't know who it was then?' said Harold, somewhat placated for not having been the first bearer of bad tidings. 'Your friend, that's who it was.'

'What friend?'

'Mrs Whatsername – Mailer. The one you said we'd have to have on the programme.'

'*Her*? Good God.' Ted took time to consider this aspect of things. 'Such a cool, fresh type she looked too.'

'Well, she won't look so fresh now,' said Harold brutally. 'She's had her head bashed in. The point is, ought we to tell them?'

'Tell who what?'

'Tell the police. About my having let it out after the amenities meeting that she was to be on the programme.'

'Did you tell people that?'

'Yes, I did. I told you at the time.'

'So you did,' said Ted, who never listened to Harold. 'You mean that could have been the reason why she got done in, I suppose. By a jealous competitor, or something.'

'Well, it could, couldn't it,' said Harold, pop-eyed with excitement. 'Murder's been done for less.'

'Fifty pee, the last one I read about,' said Ted. 'It's about the only job people are asking less for doing these days.'

'They were all livid about it when I told them,' said Harold, with relish. 'I could see by their faces.'

'Of course they were,' said Ted, thinking this was probably why Harold told them.

'Then you think I'd better go to the police about it?'

asked Harold, quivering with excitement at the thought of being taken down in shorthand by a tall, fair, fresh-faced young policeman.

'They probably know about it already,' said Ted. 'Someone's bound to have told them.'

'Spoilsport,' said Harold. 'Anyway, I'm not so sure. You know what these small places are like. People can really clam up if they want to. Especially if they feel threatened.'

'Well, go along and see them, then,' said Ted, who was pleased with any excuse for getting rid of Harold, and certainly didn't want to appear too pally with him when Joy was watching. 'Have a good chat to them. Give them the whole background.'

'I *will*,' said Harold, sliding himself off his bar stool, and giving a little wriggle at the rear, like a spaniel hoping for a walk. 'Will you hold the fort?'

'I'll hold the fort,' said Ted. 'But will Lancelot get his Guinevere?' he added in the direction of Joy Billington. She gave him a lustrous, sensual smile, and wondered vaguely who Gwen Vere was.

Inspector Parrish was profoundly embarrassed. It wasn't that he was bad at talking to children. Usually he was quite good, and all the better at it for not having to do it too often. Young criminals found him much easier than Sergeant Feather, who had all the puritanism and much of the self-righteousness of the virtuous young. But to talk to a young girl about her dead mother!

And Cressida Mailer was not making things easy for him. She was still not crying. On the surface she seemed quite collected, but Inspector Parrish noticed that her face twisted involuntarily at times, doubtless in grief or anxiety. She gave her answers calmly and briefly, as if to a history master who had asked her for the principal consequences of the Battle of Bannockburn.

'So in fact you didn't see your mother either after dinner on Monday?' said Parrish, going over ground already covered and wondering if Cressida would elaborate on her story and come up with something of value.

'No,' said Cressida, in her soft, musical voice.

'And you yourself didn't leave your own bedroom after eight o'clock except to go to the bathroom?'

'That's right,' said Cressida.

'And you were reading and writing?'

'Yes.'

'Homework, I suppose, was it?' asked Parrish. 'There's always homework, isn't there?'

'Yes, it was mostly homework,' said Cressida.

Parrish sighed. He got the impression not that the girl was trying to be unhelpful, but that she just didn't know how to be helpful. She answered by rote, as if these were matters she had pondered over long before he asked her about them.

'Where is your bedroom, now, in relation to your mother's and father's?'

Cressida answered promptly. 'It's a little box-room, right at the end of the landing. A sort of big cupboard. Mother's room was at the other end.'

'Just by the top of the stairs?'

'That's right.'

'Tell me, Cressida – can I call you that? – ' Cressida looked at him hard, and for a moment he thought she would say neither yea nor nay, but finally she smiled briefly and nodded – 'do you think your mummy could have left her room and gone out without your hearing her?'

'Yes, of course,' answered Cressida.

'You don't think you would have heard the door, or a floorboard on the stairs, or something like that?'

'I wasn't listening,' said Cressida; 'I was writing.'

'Do you always go up to your room in the evening after dinner?' asked Parrish.

'No, not always. Not if Daddy is in, or if there's anything on the television I want to watch.'

'Did Mummy often go out in the evening?' asked Parrish.

Cressida considered. 'Often? I don't know what you mean by often. Of course she went out sometimes.'

'Once a week, twice a week?'

'I can't say, really,' said Cressida. 'Often I wouldn't know – if I was in my room, like Monday night.'

'Do you know where she went?'

Cressida almost smiled. 'No, she didn't have to ask my permission.'

'She'd go and visit people, I suppose.'

'Yes, I suppose so. She had lots of friends.'

'You don't know of any particular friends that she might have gone to last night?'

'No. She was on some committee or other with Mr Jimson, I think. He lives next door.'

'Other than that –'

'No, I'm afraid I can't think of anyone.'

'What did you do yesterday morning, Cressida?'

'Yesterday morning? I helped to make Daddy's breakfast. Then I didn't feel too well, so I went back to bed for a bit. I thought I'd have the day off school.'

'You didn't think of going to ask Mummy if you could?'

'Oh no. We were quite independent, you know. She was very good, and left me alone if I wanted it. Then the policeman came – you, wasn't it? and others – and said Mother was dead. Then I stayed up and waited for Daddy.'

Parrish already felt he had got nowhere, and was likely to get nowhere.

'Is there anything you can remember that you think might help us? Anything odd that happened yesterday, or the day before. Anything out of the ordinary?'

Cressida was silent for a few moments.

'Any phone call on Monday, for example, or anything that upset Mummy at all?' Parrish became as insistent as he felt he could in the circumstances.

'No, there's nothing I can think of.'

'You will tell me if you think of anything, won't you?'

'Yes, of course. I'm trying to help as much as I can, only I don't seem to remember anything useful. Is that all?'

'Is what all? Oh yes – yes, I think so. For the moment.' Parrish had an odd feeling of having been dismissed.

'You see, Daddy is still awfully upset, and I'd like to go to him if I may.'

'That's right, you do that. Daddy must have loved Mummy very much, I can see that.'

'Of course,' said Cressida seriously. 'We both did. We're both enormously upset.'

And she left the room and went upstairs to her father.

It really isn't my day, thought Sergeant Feather. Come to that, yesterday hadn't been either, but it was nothing like as bad as today. First there had been Harold Thring. All orange-dyed hair, waving hands and seductive smile, pretending to work himself up to a great lather about his possible role in the death of Alison Mailer, and in reality hugging himself with ghoulish glee at the mere idea of it.

'Only *think*, though, Sergeant, how I must *feel*,' he had said, his mouth opening and shutting in simulated concern, making him look like a fledgling bird being fed worms. 'And of course I let slip those words, those *terrible* words, quite without thinking, *quite* without, and then to *see* the jealousy in their eyes as I did, because you *know* what people are like, and then within *minutes* maybe for all we know there she is dead by the side of the road. Well! – what a *thing* to live with, what a terrible *load* to have on your conscience.'

'I really don't think I should take it so seriously, if I were you,' Sergeant Feather had said soothingly, his hand pausing in the writing down of Harold's high-pitched story. 'In all probability there's no connection at all between the two things.'

'Oh, do you think not?' said Harold, bitterly disappointed, but grasping Feather's hand in a Victorian gesture of beseechment. '*Do* say so and put my mind at rest.'

'I'm quite sure you needn't feel responsible,' Sergeant Feather had said, trying terribly hard to retrieve his hand, locked in a distastefully clammy grip. 'Murders are not often done for a little thing like that.'

'Is that so?' said Harold, clinging like a love-sick limpet. 'But you do get such *terrible* stories in the papers these days, don't you? I'm so *glad* to learn it's not true!'

In the end Feather had had to hand him over to Sergeant Underwood, which had effectively doused his agonized conscience. Within a couple of minutes he had seen Harold prancing off down the street, and waving gaily to a passing Mrs Withens. '*Lovely* to see you, Debbie,' Harold had shouted.

And now this. If there was anything Sergeant Feather disliked and mistrusted it was characters. Local characters. Every village had one, or had to pretend to have one if it hadn't, but they were a highly dispensable element in Sergeant Feather's professional life. They were usually crooked as a corkscrew in his opinion, and he always got the notion they were taking the mickey out of him, without ever being sure how, or why. It wasn't that Stephen Feather lacked a sense of humour. He could laugh at himself with the best. But he liked to know why he was supposed to be laughing. And here was old Amos Chipweather, sitting in the most comfortable chair in the whole station (brought to him, under orders, by Feather himself) and having Parrish play up to him for nigh on half an hour in the most shameless, time-wasting fashion. The two had been going on nineteen to the dozen, and he wasn't even sure whether he was supposed to be getting all the nonsense they talked down or not.

Amos Chipweather was one of the local postmen. He wasn't a singing postman, because someone else had thought of that first, but he would do anything else on earth at the glint of a coin. The prospect of a free pint of beer would send him off into an ecstasy of scabrous rural reminiscence,

into long, improbable lectures on local lore and folk wis-
dom, or even into a tap-dance routine with a bit whistling
thrown in – all depending upon the tastes and interests of
his potential patron. Sergeant Feather thought him a shameless old scrounger, but Parrish always pointed out that he
worked hard for the driblets of charity he received, and
with an inventiveness well above the common run of mental
activity in Twytching. And because he was the sort of
character who inevitably is going to come in useful some
day, Parrish had always made it his business to cultivate
him.

'An' 'ee do say,' Amos was chuckling to Parrish, "at that
young lad from Broadwich 'at be staying at Lamb be soft
on that other furriner, Missis Billington, an' 'at he do sit
there night arter night just a-lookin' at 'er great cuddlers
a-hanging atween the pumps. I couldn't say a-self, cos I'm
too busy a-lookin' at 'em on me own account I hint got
eyes for nothing else – he-he-he-he . . .' And Amos ended
in a great wheezy guffaw, which Parrish joined in, and
the two collapsed over the table, each eyeing the other off
the while. Sergeant Feather was disgusted. This was not
the approach to the job they taught you at Police College.

'She's certainly got what it takes,' said Parrish, finally
straightening up from his frenzy of unsophisticated mirth.

'She'm got a great bullocky husband as takes it, too,'
snuffled Amos, 'and he int a goin' to let one o' them
mannikins from that there commercial radio come and
'ave 'is little bite at the cherries, I'll betcher.'

'You're probably right at that,' said Parrish. 'But it was
letters we were talking about, you remember.' He paused.
'Odd letters, letters addressed in funny ways – you know
the sort of thing I mean, don't you, Amos?'

There was an enormous, fecund rural pause.

'Oo-ah, I know what 'ee me-an,' said Amos pregnantly.

'Do you remember any, then, eh, Amos?' asked Parrish
wheedlingly.

'I remember . . .' said Amos, 'I remember a old country

saying from these 'ere parts – 'ave you 'erd it? "Thirsty
thrushes sing but gribbetty songs" – 'ave you 'erd thetn?'

'I have now,' said Parrish.

'I'se reckon I'd be but gribbetty, was I to say owt to you
now,' said Amos, putting on an expression of mock self-
doubt. "Aving this thirst on me like, after me round.'

To Stephen Feather's surprise, Inspector Parrish leant
down under his desk, unlocked his bottom drawer, and
produced a more than half-full bottle of scotch. Good
scotch at that. Cunning old bugger, thought Feather to
himself. Never said a word to me about it in all these years.
The number of times we could have done with it too, after
Saturday traffic duty and all.

'Get us a glass, Sergeant,' said Parrish rather grandly,
'and a jug of water.'

'Don't 'ee bother about no wotter,' said Amos Chipweather. 'I don't 'old with no wotter, 'cept when I 'as me
bath now and then, and better then than now is what I
ses.'

'I thought perhaps since you felt gribbetty –' suggested
Parrish.

'Nothing better 'an pure whisky for a touch of the grib-
bets,' said Amos, watching the liquid flowing into the glass,
and seeming to will a little more out of the bottle. Amos
had a very strong will.

'Now,' said Parrish, after Amos had had his first generous
sip, and had begun washing it round his large mouth with
appreciative grunts of ecstasy. 'Shoot.'

'Wew,' said Amos, swallowing finally and reluctantly,
and shaking his head as the warm shock reached his body.
'Wew, there 'ave been some oddens, I'll say that. Course,
there allus be oddens, what wi' some folk's 'andwritin', and
little kiddies as writes to God and the Queen, and that.
But there 'ave been a powerful few oddens goin' through
this 'ere office in these last weeks.'

'What sort of oddens?' said Parrish encouragingly.

'Wew,' said Amos, 'most on 'ems quite simple like, see.

Thems as 'as sent them's just cut a line or two out of the drectry.'

'The telephone drectry?' asked Parrish.

'That's 'er,' said Amos. 'Just the one line, in some cases. But them as 'as businesses, like, and 'as it writ large on them there pages at the back, thems a bit larger. Just cut out, they was, an' stuck on to th'emvelope wi' that there sticky stuff what gets all around yer fingers and doesn't go where yer puts it.'

'Sellotape?' asked Parrish.

'That's 'er,' said Amos. 'Just stuck on wi' sellytape, they was. Then there was others –'

'Different types?'

'Aaaah. Themses was like print. Single letters, like, one after another. Only not like 'ee or I'ud write – a bit topsy-piggledy, like. No, these was all reg'lar and shipshape, like 'im as writ used a sort o' shape to trace 'em out, like.'

'One of those child's lettering sets, do you mean?'

'Oh-ah. 'Appen. Int had no children goin' on for fifty years now – not as I'se 'ad the bringin' up on.'

Amos's old face creased with delicious rumination, and he finished the final drops of his scotch.

'Now, what about the details,' said Parrish. 'Who were these letters addressed to, can you remember that?'

He already knew the answer to that. Amos's wrist started jiggling his glass from side to side, and his disreputable old eye cast meaningful glances in its direction.

'Aaah, if only I could,' he said. 'But a man's memory do get powerful mumbled at this hour of the day.'

Parrish poured.

'Aaaah,' said Amos, as if tasting liquid for the first time after a prolonged drought, 'that do be better. Wew then, who was it now? Tain't easy to call 'em to mind, not wi' all the work and responsibilities we 'ave, like Mr Jackson says. Let's see. There was that niminy-piminy schoolteacher type wi' the nasty flummoxin' ways kiddies hate, and wi' the bonny wife.'

'Mr Jimson?' suggested Parrish.

'Oh-ah, that's 'im,' said Amos Chipweather.

'When did he get one?'

'Ooo, 'appen a fortnight ago, 'appen longer. Can't rightly figure out the details. Then there was 'im at the Lamb wi' the frogglessome wife, and 'er as keeps the shop – Mrs Leaze.'

'And the vicar?' prompted Parrish.

'Oh-ah. Them there clergies get in everywhere they int a-wanted. 'E 'ad one, yes, I 'member that. Who else? Wew, Mrs Buller, she 'ad one, and 'er daughter as keeps 'aving the population explosions – yes, that I do mind. And Mr Mailer –'

'Mr Mailer?' said Parrish, immediately interested.

'Oh-ah. Or were it 'er as got it? Can't rightly remember that.' Amos furrowed his brow, and seemed genuinely distressed at not being able to deliver the goods. 'No, I can't call it to mind.'

'When was it, can you remember that?'

'Can't rightly, not seein' as there's bin so many. Wasn't one of th' early ones, more recent than that, but they be all frumbled up in me mind, like. Last one was that Edgar chap from school, I do mind that. That were yesterday, so it's fresh, like.'

'Yesterday,' said Parrish thoughtfully. 'I see. What about today, then?'

'No, int bin no more today?'

'Have there been many days without any in the past few weeks, or do they come in little rushes, so to speak.'

'Oh-ah, there int bin that many,' said Amos. "Appen two or three days 'd go by wi'out one. 'Appen more. But I don't call to mind any day when there was more than one, not on my round.'

'And there's no one else got one, that you can remember?'

Amos furrowed his brow, and entered gradually into a

prolonged bout of rural contemplation, emerging struggling at the end of it to shake his head regretfully.

'Int no more I can think on. 'Appen there was others, but I can't call 'em to mind. I'll ask me mates, o' course . . .'

Parrish, encouraging hand on shoulder, showed Amos out, suggesting that they would always be there if he ever remembered anything else that might be of use, however slight. The two parted most affectionately.

'You'll have him down here every hour of the day,' observed Sergeant Feather sourly when he came back. 'Old scrounger – he'll remember that one had the stamp stuck on upside down, and he'll come snuffling round for another drink.'

'Case'll be in the bag by Saturday,' said Parrish comfortably. 'Anyway, I've had that two years – time I got a fresh supply.'

'I can't see how you can be so confident we'll have anyone charged by Saturday,' said Feather.

'Broadwich are playing home,' murmured Parrish. His sergeant ignored him.

'Anonymous letters are the very devil,' said Feather, remembering an earlier case. 'People sit on them like broody hens, swear they never received one, swear they burned it as soon as they'd read it, swear they never opened it at all. I've known it take a week to get an anonymous letter out of someone, and then it was only a lot of words I learnt before I took the eleven-plus.'

'I'm hoping these are a bit more interesting than that,' said Parrish. His cunning old eyes glinted. 'And I doubt if they'll be as reluctant as all that this time. There'll be all the usual fuss and palaver at the beginning, but eventually I wouldn't mind betting folk will bring them out pretty sharpish.'

'Why should they?'

'Murder, that's why. Folk around here may be slow, but

they're not completely dim. They'll have made the connection: anonymous letters – murder. And having made it, they'll be scared rigid: either they might be done in, or they might be accused of it – revenge on the letter-writer. Once it gets through to them that we know they've received one, I should think they'll co-operate, with a bit of pressure.'

Sergeant Feather thought this out. 'You mean they'll think the letters were a sort of preliminary, the appetiser, so to speak, with the murder as the main course to follow?'

'Something of the sort. Or else that Alison Mailer wrote them, and got herself done in by one of the recipients. But we'll stress the first possibility – tell them she received one herself. Then they'll be scared stiff for their own skins, and we'll promise them full police protection if they co-operate.'

Stephen was still deep in thought. 'Interesting,' he said, 'that there was no letter today. Of course we'll have to wait a bit, but if they've stopped, then the thing will be fairly clear, as far as I can see.'

'Yes, interesting,' said Parrish, 'if a trifle obvious. No, I don't rule out Alison Mailer as the writer, and certainly I don't rule her out because either she or her husband got one. We'll keep her in mind, as they say. But it's not half as open and shut as you seem to think. By the way – how did she get on the programme?'

'What?'

'You told me that little orange-haired birdie said he'd let it out on Monday night that she was to be on the programme.'

'Yes.'

'How did she get on?'

Stephen looked crestfallen. 'I didn't ask him that.'

'Oh my God,' said Parrish disgusted. 'Talk about keeping a dog and having to do the rat-catching yourself.'

'Well, he was talking such a lot of bilge,' said Stephen in an aggrieved voice, 'and then he kept fluttering those damned eyelashes at me, and he grabbed hold of my hand, and I – '

But Parrish had left the room, closing the door with the nearest such an equable type could get to a bang.

CHAPTER IX

PRIVATE AND PERSONAL

The rest of Wednesday, and most of Thursday morning as well, was devoted by Parrish to the securing of the mysterious correspondence which had apparently floated around Twytching for the past few weeks without anyone being willing to divulge to anyone else the fact of his having received one. This was a job Parrish felt he had to do for himself. Sergeant Feather's more brutal and censorious approaches seemed more likely to scare people into silence than to encourage them into full co-operation. However, he let him loose on Mrs Buller's Val, with strict instructions to be understanding and lovable. And – feeling much more guilty about this – he gave the vicar to Sergeant Underwood, on the grounds that he had had enough of religious dottiness to last him for several months. The rest of Amos Chipweather's list of lucky recipients he took himself.

It was not quite as easy a job as he had hoped. The letters, whatever their qualities as literature, had certainly managed to scare their recipients to death. A hunted look came into their torpid rustic eyes at the most oblique reference to such a thing as an anonymous letter. Some even feigned ignorance of the term. The whole operation therefore involved a great deal of patient toing and froing, of letting assurances sink in gradually, of convincing people that others were in the same boat, and that much the safest course would be to hand the letters over at once in return for police protection. Oddly enough, the recipient he visited first was the hardest nut to crack. He had always thought of Mrs Leaze as an amiable old crook, as incapable of secrecy as your average Labour cabinet minister. But for once in her life she seemed to have been shocked into silence. Like most of the rest she denied vigorously for the whole of Parrish's first visit that she had received any such letter :

'If you believe that old scrounger Amos Chipweather, a dirty old rogue as reads people's postcards and pinches kiddies' postal orders at Christmas, then you want your 'ead reading,' she said. 'It's a wonder to me why we should pay our rates to support a police force that can't mind its own business better than that.'

On his second visit, fear had conquered shyness, and she admitted to having received such a letter a week or ten days before. No power on earth would make her show it to the Inspector, however. In fact, like every single one of the other recipients, she insisted that she had burnt it.

'You know me, Inspector,' she said. 'I'm never one to gossip and pry into other people's lives, and if all I 'ear is true some of 'em wouldn't stand up to much prying, that's sure as sure, and when you get some nasty-minded soul as 'as got so little to do that 'e can sit down and put together a letter like that, well, I feel like I feel when someone comes into my shop and wants to spread filthy tales about other people in this village. What I do is I shut 'em up, and what I did with this was I burnt it.'

'Very natural, I'm sure, Mrs Leaze,' said Parrish, not believing a word. 'You said the letter was "put together" – wasn't it written in the normal way?'

'No, it wasn't. Them things never are, are they? It was some words clipped from newspapers and such likes, sometimes just the one word, sometimes two or three together. Then some of the words were typewritten like –'

'Typewritten?'

'Well, sort of typewritten. Typewritten and yet not typewritten, if you see what I mean.'

'Not exactly,' said Parrish. 'What precisely did they look like?'

But Mrs Leaze's descriptive powers were exhausted, and he could get no more revealing description of it than that. When he turned to the contents of the letters, her initial caginess returned in full.

'I wouldn't dignify it by repeating it,' said Mrs Leaze, drawing herself up to her full bulk. 'I threw it straight in the fire, so I 'ardly saw what was in it. In any case there was nothing whatsoever that could interest you.'

Deciding that these statements contained the seeds of mutual contradiction Parrish pressed her further, but when he did finally succeed in getting something out of her, it was decidedly vague, and must be, Parrish decided, very much less colourful than the original.

'It said I was a filthy-minded old – well, I won't soil my lips,' said Mrs Leaze, 'and you know me, Inspector, and you can vouch that gossip never sullies this shop no matter what folks 'ave done, and do it they will, as you well know. Then there was something silly about buying up old stock and stuff about to go off and selling it at full price.'

'No!' said Inspector Parrish.

'Yes!' said Mrs Leaze. 'Well, you can see yourself 'ow daft that is. 'Snot as though Twytching was London, where folks don't know the difference between a fresh lettuce and a month-old one, is it? Little country place like this people know exactly what they're buying in the way of vegetables and eggs and that, stands to reason. I wouldn't last a week if I tried that sort of trick, I can tell you.'

Mrs Leaze's confident protestations rather ignored the fact that she had little or no competition in Twytching. And Parrish did not think of Twytchingites as being particularly close to the soil (close to the telly would be nearer the truth), or as anything other than slovenly shoppers who could be deceived by the most patently bogus special offer, the most obviously inflated packaging device. However,

Parrish felt there were enough people around these days acting as the shopper's friend without the police getting involved, so he concentrated on prising the letter out of Mrs Leaze. It proved to be more than his powers of persuasion could achieve. Neither sweet understanding nor his standard majesty-of-the-law pose could come near to breaking down her flabby immovability.

'I said I burnt it, and burnt it I did, and there's an end of it. If you don't believe me then I'm sorry for you, and 'ope you'll learn in time the difference between an honest soul as works for 'er living and chapel twice on Sunday if it's fine and them liars and criminals you 'ave to deal with every day of the week. You 'ave to dirty your 'ands with them and I pity you for it, but I int going to be treated as one such myself, I assure you.'

'Did the letter contain a threat?' Parrish asked unabashed.

'A threat?'

'Or a demand for money?'

'Money? There's little enough money to be got out of me. 'Aven't you 'eard 'ow difficult things are for the small shopkeeper?' Mrs Leaze's eyes strayed involuntarily round the room, but unfortunately they caught sight of the enormous and expensive fur coat, hanging ostentatiously in the hall. She quickly changed the subject. 'As to threats – well, there was something silly about mending my ways. What was it : "Stop flaunting yourself around Twytching" – me, at my age, flaunting, I ask you – "as if you own the place. Mend your ways and cease cheating and swindling or exposure and public ignominy will ensure." '

' "Ensue", I suppose,' murmured Parrish.

'No, there was nothing said about suing,' said Mrs Leaze.

But Parrish noted she could remember the letter well enough when it suited her.

Parrish finally got to see Tom Billington an hour or so before opening time, and found Ted Livermore scuttling upstairs to his room after a hard afternoon of bogus local historians and cakes of unique Twytching recipe. Ted was beginning to think that for sheer nullity and tedium the Twytching documentary would be nigh unsurpassable.

'You don't want me, Inspector, do you?' he asked Parrish, pausing on the stairs.

'Not really, sir,' said Parrish. 'It's Mr Billington I'm after. But there was just one thing my sergeant forgot to ask your . . . assistant producer would you call him?'

'I'm surprised there was anything my assistant forgot to tell *him*,' said Ted. 'Harold in confidential mood is pretty voluminous as a rule.'

'Well, I believe he did go fairly fully into his role in the matter,' said Parrish, grinning briefly. 'And we tried to re-assure him about that. But he didn't tell us why she was on the programme.'

'Who? Mrs Mailer?'

'That's right, sir. She didn't seem quite the type you normally use. She wasn't greatly involved with things locally.'

'Wasn't she?' said Ted, this not having been quite the impression Alison had given him. Then the penny dropped. 'Oh, I see – I suppose you must think that I slept with her, do you?'

Inspector Parrish was unperturbed. 'The thought had crossed my mind, sir.'

'Wrong, I'm afraid, Inspector. Wrong, for once. No – she did come along to see me in my office some weeks ago, and Harold *was* down here on a reconnaissance trip, but I'm afraid we both kept our clothes on the whole time, which would probably surprise some of the old tabbies around here.'

'Perhaps,' said Parrish, 'though I must say Mrs Mailer hadn't the reputation locally for sleeping around.'

'No, she didn't strike me as a compulsive spring-tester,' said Ted. 'The fact is, she's a friend of the BWC.'

'BWC, sir?'

'Big White Chief. Otherwise Sir Charles Watson, our principal shareholder – the man who holds the purse-strings. When she heard we were going to Twytching she just tripped along and introduced herself to me – without any ulterior motive in the world, of course.'

'Did the . . . er . . . BWC bring her along himself, or did he send a letter of introduction?'

'No, he just sort of sent her along, I imagine.'

'You didn't check later?'

'Did Moses ask for a replay of the Ten Commandments?' said Ted. 'No, I just accepted what she said. We chewed the cud for a bit about Twytching, what a boring little place it was, and so on, and finally I did the expected and offered her a spot on the programme. And after a bit of hesitation, she accepted.'

'Genuine hesitation?'

'Of course not. But better done than usual.'

'Well, thank you, sir. I won't keep you.'

'Will you be with Mr Billington for long?'

'Some time, I'm afraid. It's a rather ticklish matter I've got to discuss with him.'

'I'll warn his wife,' said Ted helpfully. 'So long, Inspector.'

Tom Billington certainly did make heavy weather of the whole thing. He sat on the old sofa in the public bar, simmering and glowering, as if the strength of his feelings could find no sufficient utterance in mere words. Quite apart from anything else, the receipt of the letter had distressed him because he had thought he was accepted in Twytching. He was unaware of the fifty-year probation period imposed on newcomers to the village, and he had thought that because the locals came to drink his beer they had taken him to their bosoms as one of themselves. But they drank his beer because it was good, and they kept rigidly to the thousand and one nice gradations of language, attitude and behaviour by which a proper distinction could be drawn between a 'Twytcher' and one less favoured by nature. It was a dim realization of this fact that lay behind Tom Billington's heavy obstructiveness.

'Was a right nasty piece of work, it was,' he said, when he had finally, after half an hour of persuasion, admitted to having received an anonymous letter. 'That sort of bloke ought to be locked away. They're psycho, that's what they are.'

'I think you're probably right,' said Parrish. 'On the other hand, there could be some quite different mind or motive behind it – something really cunning. Possibly something connected with this murder. That's why I want to see one – '

'I burnt it,' Tom blurted out quickly.

' – to check on the typewriter and that sort of thing. We haven't a hope of getting whoever did it and putting a stop to it unless we see some of the actual letters.'

'I burnt it,' said Tom, rather more slowly. He shifted his enormous wrestler's weight around the sofa, uneasy.

'And the reason I'm relying on you, is that you're a stranger. You know as well as I do that here in Twytching everybody's business is public business. You've only got to pick your nose, and it's commented on. That's why none of the natives will show me the letters they got. Too many old skeletons in the woodshed, so to speak. Now you, coming from outside, you're above all this. You're outside this long saga of gossip and tongue-wagging. And of course in your job you want to stay on the right side of the police . . .'

'I burnt it,' said Tom, but rather as if Umbaba the Wild Man from Borneo had his arms and legs in grips of steel, and was bashing his face against the canvas. 'That's what I did.'

'Have you thought,' asked Parrish, 'how grateful folk around here will be if it's you who shows the letter? That's the sort of thing that helps a newcomer in a closed-in little place like this. Quite apart from the fact that it will show us you've got nothing to hide.'

'I 'ave got nothing to hide,' said Tom. 'It was just a load of filf, that's all it was.'

'And of course the contents will be as secret as the grave as far as we're concerned,' said Parrish. 'You can just tell people you handed it over to us, and leave it at that.'

Tom Billington raised his weight from the sofa, and lumbered over to a shelf behind the bar. Taking up a bottle of a seldom drunk liqueur, he extracted a piece of paper from under it, and came slowly back, still obviously pondering.

'Since you put it like that,' he said finally, 'I suppose people will be pleased if it's me who stumps up. Take the pressure off them, like. And you can see what a load of old cods it is.'

He methodically unfolded the sheet of paper, and read it over to himself, glowering dully. Then he spread it out slowly over the table between them, and Parrish was able to read :

'Filthy foreigners like you ought TO BE SHOT,' said the note. 'Bringing your loose LONDON morals and parading your shameless COW of a wife for every vile lecher in the VILLAGE who wants to fuck her, and turning your pub into a male brothel. Don't try and push yourself forward or you will both be EX-POSED as a whore and a cuckold. Be warned and keep quiet.'

'Well,' said Parrish. 'What a good vocabulary. Shows what a liberal education can do for you.'

'The foul fiend,' proclaimed the vicar to Sergeant Underwood, spluttering his fricatives like a burning chip-pan, 'the foul fiend must have a hand in it. Whence can such rank disease of the mind spring, but from him, whence but from him such aberrations of the intellect, such sores and abscesses of the spirit?'

Sergeant Underwood admired the air of perpetual lunatic sermonizing which characterized the vicar's speech, but she recollected that the police had to be interested in a source for the letters more immediate than the foul fiend.

'With your knowledge of the parish,' she said, 'you surely must have some idea who has that sort of imagination.'

'Who can tell?' neighed the vicar, characteristically throwing his glances at the far ceiling. 'Nobody. Everybody. Where can Satan *not* implant himself, force entry, penetrate? Yet there are here some who are mine enemies – '

'Thine enemies – I mean your?' stumbled Sergeant Underwood.

'But I will stay my hand. Vengeance is not mine, but the Lord's. There shall be silence in heaven about the space of half an hour. Or longer.'

'Don't you think in view of the – '

'Meanwhile,' went on the vicar, 'in the interim, I have made contact with the woman Mailer.'

'Made contact?' repeated Sergeant Underwood, puzzled.

'Last night,' said the vicar nonchalantly, 'after a prolonged wrestling of the spirit.'

Sergeant Underwood dimly remembered having heard that the vicar was reputed by the more credulous of his parishioners to be possessed of supernatural powers, and that he himself claimed abilities akin to those of the lady who communicates with Beethoven and Bernard Shaw and brings back from her encounters symphonies and witticisms so inferior to those written while they were alive as to suggest that death is not all it's cracked up to be.

'What did you ask Mrs Mailer?' asked Sergeant Underwood.

'I asked her,' said the vicar, 'if it were she who had committed to paper this slanderous ordure.'

'And what did she reply?'

'She said the carpets in her heavenly mansion were incredibly bourgeois. Disappointing in the circumstances. But I shall work at it.'

'Of course normally,' said Timothy Jimson, 'I would have taken something like this straight to the police.'

Jean Jimson watched her husband closely, with the absolute knowledge born out of the terrible propinquity of marriage. He was expanding his little body pompously, as if to meet an attack, but she read plainly underneath the outward bellicosity, signs of fear, panic – perhaps something else too, even nastier than she had ever expected.

'Quite right, sir,' said Parrish, settling himself comfortably down into an armchair, but finding his posterior getting poked by a piece of Meccano. 'Exactly what everybody ought to do. Why didn't you in this case?'

'Living in Twytching, Inspector,' said Jimson, as if this was to be the beginning of a lengthy exposition, 'is not like living in a city. None of that blessed anonymity here! You have to remember that a schoolmaster is in a peculiarly delicate, peculiarly *perilous* position. The least breath of scandal and he is in jeopardy – his career, his way of life, his standing in the school, in the community. School-teaching is not like other jobs, and we are very much in the position of doctors, clergymen, people of that kind.' A memory of the vicar of Twytching came through Timothy's mind, and he decided to hurry on with his argument. 'All this is understandable, of course, absolutely understandable. Don't get me wrong – I wouldn't have it any other way. Parents are quite right to insist on the highest possible standards – nothing disgusts me more than this fashionable slovenliness – dress, haircut, speech, accent! Some of the accents one hears nowadays among the younger staff members –'

'Yes, but you were saying, sir,' interposed Parrish.

'Quite, yes, well, I felt that though I have of course the highest respect for you, and your discretion, none more so, I don't know your subordinates. You yourself must agree that the police force is in the same boat as the rest of the professions these days: the difficulty is recruiting men of the right calibre. Now for all I know one of your constables could have broadcast the whole damned thing around town – in fact, for all I know one of them could be an old pupil of mine. You see my problem.'

Timothy Jimson's harangue reminded Parrish of Sergeant Feather in his more self-righteous moods, and he thought idly how gratified Stephen would be to hear the police force described as a profession. But he felt the need to put in a word to defend the integrity of his subordinates, which was in fact one thing about them he was fairly confident of.

'I can assure you, sir,' he said, thrusting his hand into the seat of his chair to remove another piece of Meccano, and finding it suddenly encountering a half-sucked sweet, 'that nothing of the kind would have happened. My people understand their job.'

'Well, of course, I accept your reassurances, Inspector,' said Timothy, 'but I think you ought to remember how everyone loves to find out anything discreditable about schoolteachers. Any little scandal of that sort goes straight into the *News of the World,* with the word "schoolmaster" blazoned in the headline. People hate us, you know. Jealousy, of course, but it's a fact of life we all have to live with in my profession.'

'Well, now, sir,' said Parrish, assuming the majesty-of-the-law pose that he thought might work with Jimson, who seemed to be both aware of his duties as a citizen and a coward to boot (majesty-of-the-law poses only worked with the respectable or the would-be respectable), 'I hope you'll make up for this dereliction of duty, which I'm willing to overlook just this once, by handing over the letter without any more fuss. If you'd done it earlier you would have saved us a great deal of trouble, perhaps even prevented worse than that.'

There was a long silence. Timothy Jimson was wrestling

with his conscience. Or possibly weighing the pros and cons. Jean watched him, intensely interested. She had never seen him in this sort of situation before. She knew her place better than to say a word.

'Very well, Inspector,' said Timothy, and with a reluctance that was palpable to everyone else in the room he went over to the sideboard and opened the door. A large mass of building bricks, jigsaw puzzles, story-books and games cascaded to the floor, and spoilt the attempted nobility of his gesture.

'I've been meaning to tidy that out,' said Jean.

Timothy did not honour this with a reply, but opened one of the drawers, rummaged to the bottom, and finally produced a sheet of paper, which he did not look at. He stalked over to Parrish and handed it over to him.

'You'll see for yourself,' he said, 'that it's obviously someone's dirty-minded fantasies.'

Parrish smoothed it open, and read:

'KEEP under cover or the whole town will know that you molest little girls after school *and* commit fornication, adultery and all uncleanliness with girls under the AGE OF CONSENT. People like you should not be ALLOWED near the children of DECENT folk. Watch your STEP.'

Parrish studied it carefully. It looked very like the similar message addressed to Tom Billington. Though short, it took up the entire page, because some of the words were in large capitals – in some cases obviously newspaper headlines, in others (such as the words 'age of consent') apparently of stiffer materials, possibly from a paperback book. Other words were typewritten, but close inspection revealed that these were photocopies rather than originals. That was no doubt what Mrs Leaze was trying to get at. Parrish puzzled his head over these. He didn't see that the fact that these were photocopies would absolutely prevent the lab people identifying the typewriter they came from, should it turn up. Did the writer think it would? Most of the rest of the words were simply cut from newspapers, several different ones apparently, though there was one rather unattractive type that seemed to predominate.

'You don't have the envelope?' said Parrish, turning to Timothy Jimson and observing that his face was deeply flushed.

'No, I don't,' snapped Timothy. 'I threw it away without thinking. Human factor, I'm afraid.'

'I see,' said Parrish. 'Well, of course we take it for granted this is someone's sick fantasy. But I'm most grateful to you for showing it to me finally. It will help us considerably.'

'Can we throw it in the fire now?' said Timothy, without much hope in his voice.

'Certainly not,' said Parrish, taking it up carefully and preparing to bear it off. 'But if we ever need to use it, you can be quite sure we shall not reveal the exact contents.'

As Parrish left the room, wrapped in his comfortable rural dignity, Jean Jimson watched her husband. His eyes were watching Parrish's movements with an odd mingling of fear, dislike and contempt. Suddenly he became aware that he was being watched, and he visibly pulled himself together.

'Nasty little episode,' he said. 'Much too like a third-rate play for my liking. Clear up this mess, can't you, Jean?'

After her initial hesitations, those hesitations which all the recipients seemed to feel were demanded by etiquette, Val Rice (whose married surname seemed so dispensable that she remained to everyone in Twytching Mrs Buller's Val) became as obliging in this matter as she customarily was in most others. At the beginning of the interview, which took place in her council house living-room, overlooked by china poodles and brass animals of indeterminate species, she had cleverly seated Sergeant Feather on the sofa, though he had aimed himself at an upright chair. So when she fetched the letter, still in its envelope, she was able to sit beside him, and as she got close to read the letter over with him she pressed her bulging belly against him in a manner which Sergeant Feather, trying desperately to be verbal rather than instinctive, mentally described as 'suggestive'.

"Course, it's only some silly old sex-maniac,' she said, digging him in the ribs, 'and I've known enough of that type in my time, so it's not as though I'm bothered.'

In spite of his efforts, Sergeant Feather felt himself becoming hot and red, and he wished he hadn't seated himself in the corner of the sofa, whence retreat was impracticable. He looked down, trying rather too hard to be sublimely unaware of such things as bulging bellies and shapely legs. She did have shapely legs. Very shapely legs. Val crossed them as she fished in the envelope.

'My Sam's doing a job for someone,' she said irrelevantly. Sergeant Feather concentrated on the envelope. The envelope. Concentrate on the envelope. Beautiful even capitals, drawn with a . . . Concentrate on the envelope. Drawn with a lettering set.

'This is it,' said Val, smoothing it out lovingly over Sergeant Feather's worsted-clad thighs. 'In all its glory! What a mind, eh? What a mind!'

The letter read:

'Your type is a disgrace to the TOWN. You walk round inviting men to SCREW YOU! Anyone with an ounce of shame would have left years ago, and taken that ginger-haired little bastard with you. Nymphomaniacs like you who have sexual relationships with MEN all over the town ought to WATCH IT. Other PEOPLE get hurt and might HURT back. You and your men are like pigs barbecued in your own shit.'

'Dear me,' said Sergeant Feather.

'Actually,' said Mrs Buller's Val, leaning seductively across Sergeant Feather, and gazing invitingly into his eyes, 'there's ginger hair in Sam's family. Several generations back.'

Assembled together they were a pretty impressive bunch, though as with most things of that kind, with prolonged reading a feeling of monotony was liable to set in. The style was rather jerky, due no doubt to the difficulty of finding the desired word in newspapers and other convenient sources. At times, in fact, one got the impression that the author had given up striving for *le mot juste* and had taken whatever unpleasant *mot* had come most readily to hand. Certainly he hadn't found anything very interesting to say to Mrs Buller, for one, so that the message to her concentrated largely on the delinquencies of her nearest and dearest, which she was accused of aiding and abetting. That to Jack Edgar accused him of being a 'personal screwing machine' and a 'masculine whore'. ('Good gracious,' said Sergeant Underwood.) It was clear, thought Inspector Parrish, that Mr Edgar was regarded by the writer as another of Harold Thring's conquests, unless there were other potential clients for masculine whores in Twytching. What havoc Harold's eyelashes seemed to wreak! That to the vicar was more specific. Sergeant Underwood blushed as she handed it over. She had been a regular attendant at Sunday School in the little village she came from, and there the vicar had been regarded with a truly Victorian awe. The writer of the note was far from sharing such feelings. Having told him succinctly that he was a geriatric case and a disgrace to his cloth, it went on to say he was useless for anything 'except producing ginger-HAIRED little buggers and COPULATING in the vestry with girls from the CHOIR'.

'I always wondered why people used to shake their heads over that boy,' said Sergeant Feather.

'Anyone who was a real policeman would have found

out years ago,' said Parrish grumpily. 'Well, tell us, lad, was she worth the vicar's immortal soul?'

Stephen Feather blushed deeply. Parrish looked back at the array of filth spread out on the table.

'Odd letters,' he said after a pause.

'No demands for money,' pointed out Sergeant Underwood. 'So it doesn't seem to have been blackmail.'

'No – but that often comes later. Send one or two of these little marvels, then start making demands when they're thoroughly frightened.'

'He can hardly have hoped to get anything out of Val Rice,' pointed out Sergeant Underwood. 'It's not as though she had any reputation to keep up. The whole town knows about that boy.'

'Except Stephen,' said Parrish. 'And then there's the two schoolmasters. Everyone knows teachers earn less in a month than an illegal immigrant in his first fortnight. As far as extracting money is concerned schoolmasters are very poor bets.'

'Jimson has some private money, I believe,' said Sergeant Feather, pleased to have got away from the subject of Val Rice.

'Really?' said Parrish. 'How do you know?'

'I was in his class at Barstowe Grammar. That's what they said when he bought that house. It's a bit out of his class.'

'Better go into that. By the bye, if you were in his class, you'd better be silent as the grave about that letter. He says it was that sort of possibility that stopped him coming to us with it in the first place.'

'I'm not in the habit of spreading official matters through the town,' said Stephen priggishly.

'We'd better hand these little darlings over to the experts once you've typed the transcripts,' said Parrish. 'I suppose this is about the lot, except for the Mailer one.'

'You didn't get on to him, then?'

'No. I thought I'd give him another day to get over things. Anyway, the boys who are going over his house won't have finished till tomorrow. If anything comes out of that I'll kill two birds. Of course we have no guarantees it was to him, and if it was to his wife, I'd bet she wouldn't have told him of it.'

Parrish paused. He had been looking carelessly down at the letters spread out on the table, and now he took off his glasses and bent close to them, peering.

'Odd that,' he said finally.

'What?'

'Those words that have been typed and photocopied. Can you see? They've been cut out differently from the others.'

The two sergeants bent to look closely, bumped their heads together and went off into interminable apologies before diving carefully towards the letters again. Finally they stood up.

'Don't see it,' said Sergeant Feather. 'They're all cut out with scissors, aren't they? They all look the same to me.'

'Look again, man,' said Parrish testily. 'Look at the corners. Now do you see?'

'Well,' said Feather, after prolonged observation and an effort to think that seemed to tick through the silent room, 'they sort of go in.'

'Exactly. Where?'

'At the top, at both ends.'

'Precisely. The others are cut more or less square, right angles at each corner, and so on. But the typed ones are all cut at a slant inwards, from bottom to top. Why?'

The other two thought hard.

'Can't imagine,' said Stephen. 'But it can't be important.'

'Thank you, Dr Watson,' said Parrish. 'You may return to your practice.'

CHAPTER X

IN QUEST OF A PERSONALITY

The information from the various police experts came through to Parrish in dribs and drabs. The medical evidence on Alison was suggestive, but wide open to a variety of interpretations. The time of death was probably some time between about eight and eleven on Monday evening – and the doctors wanted to leave those outer limits as vague as could be. Like all professionals they left as many openings as possible to avoid being proved wrong. Alison had been hit twice on the back of the head, low down where the skull was most vulnerable. Once she had been hit with a flat, heavy instrument of some kind, once with what might have been something thinner and sharper but which was probably the edge of the same flat instrument as caused the other blow. Whether she was merely stunned by the first, or killed, was not clear, nor could it be stated for certain whether she had been killed where she was found or elsewhere. There was dirt in the wound, but this proved little. Some degree of strength had been necessary to administer the blows, but little above the ordinary. Alison's skull, like so much else about her, was brittle.

The experts' report on the letters came through very quickly. There were no fingerprints on any of them, other than the recipients'. The provenance of the words had caused no great problems. Most of them had been cut from newspapers, the majority from the pages of the *Daily Telegraph*, but many from the *News of the World*, the *Sun*, and others. There were some words from the covers of paperback books (for example, *Age of Consent*) and a few which seemed to come from the inside of an unidentified paperback. The typewriter used for the typed words had

probably been an Olivetti Lettera 36, and the words had
been copied on a Rank Xerox machine, one of the less expensive varieties. The only envelope, that shown to Feather
by Mrs Buller's Val, was of the same cheap Woolworth's
brand as the paper, and was postmarked 'Twytching, April
16th'. This seemed to have been one of the earliest letters,
possibly the earliest, since the others remembered theirs as
coming later in the month or in the course of May. Jack
Edgar's had been the last, coming second post on Tuesday,
May 21st, the day after the amenities meeting and the
murder of Alison Mailer. It had probably been posted late
on the Monday night, another suggestive fact.

'By the way,' said Inspector Parrish to Jack Edgar,
meeting him in the street on Friday morning when he was
on his way to Arnold Mailer's, 'I suppose you must have
met Harold Thring, the little birdie from Radio Broadwich.'

Jack Edgar was a tall, well-built chap, with an incipient
paunch, the result of a typically Twytching indolence. He
had rather sleazy good looks, and thought himself irresistible. At parties his unending stream of sexy innuendoes and
dirty snickers was variously received, as were his incessantly
roving hands. Some of his adolescent girl pupils fell in love
with him, but none of the brighter ones did. He showed
no signs of being embarrassed by Parrish's question, and
seemed a model of airy frankness.

'Harold? But of course! Who in Twytching hasn't met
our own little Harold by now?'

'Where did you meet him, sir?'

'At the meeting of the Jimson fan club – what do they
call themselves? The Amenities Group, that's right. He sat
next to me. I was favoured, you might say.' He gave a
fruity chuckle. 'Our Harold gave every sign of being smitten
by my charms, but so far there haven't been any results –
not in the form of an invitation to stardom on his dreary
little documentary, anyway. I am downcast, needless to
say.'

He spread out his hand in an Italianate gesture of grief.

Inspector Parrish thought he probably was downcast.

'You say he gave every sign, sir. May I ask . . .'

'Shall we just say my roving hands have met their match at last, Inspector?' said Jack Edgar with a greasy smirk.

'Was there anyone sitting near you who could have seen Mr Thring's . . . approaches, shall we call them?' asked Inspector Parrish.

'I suppose so,' said Jack. 'If they could manage to wrench their attention away from my fellow pedagogue's dazzling discourse. Unlikely, but just in the realms of the possible. Let's see.' He considered. 'There was no one behind us, and only Mrs Brewer directly in front – I remember the whiff. She was concentrating on the meeting with exemplary attention – somewhat studied, perhaps, but exemplary. I doubt if she saw anything. Wait a tick – there was little Miss Potts from the County Library at the other end of the row, with nobody in between us. Then – that's right – I think Jimson may have seen us from the stage. I thought Harold's little attentions put him off his stride during his opening address. May be my imagination, but I had a good chuckle over it at the time.'

'Well, thank you, sir,' said Parrish, rather glad he had no children to blossom under the influence of Mr Edgar. 'You've been very helpful.'

Parrish pursued his way past the Lamb and Child, where the Broadwich Broadcasting recording van was drawn up. There was a great deal of fussing going on, with Ted in the middle of it, and standing in the doorway of the Lamb, talking to Tom Billington, was the newly-arrived interviewer from the Wisconsin station. Hank Nelson was a very large middle-aged man, with a dreadful freshness about him. He was wearing an immaculate light-weight suit, and a great expanse of white shirt. He had a tan too perfect for nature, and this seemed somehow to cast doubt on the authenticity of the chest. He had a splendid smile imprinted on his face, and he seemed intent on living up to the stereotype American of everyone's imagination. 'It's all so fantastically *English*!' he was saying to Tom. Harold, gazing wistfully, said to no one in particular: 'He must have been dishy, twenty years ago!' Soon, Parrish imagined, when the lethargic curiosity of the assembled Twytchingites was appeased, Hank would retreat with Tom and Joy into the snug bar, and they would all record an interview in which the cockney proprietors would say what a charming little place Twytching was, how friendly all the locals were, how beautiful the countryside around, and in general how close an approximation to the life of our First Fathers in Paradise was lived by the inhabitants there. Parrish shook his head dubiously, and went on his way.

Arnold Mailer's eyes had grey lines around them, but otherwise he seemed calm enough. He was in his study, away from the activities of the team of men who had let Parrish into the house and who were nearing the end of their job of taking the place apart. Cressida left the study when the Inspector was shown in, smiling briefly and rather beautifully. She had her mother's looks and self-possession, thought Parrish as he watched her go, though not her complacency.

From his reaction to Parrish's first question it would seem as though nothing could have been further from Arnold Mailer's expectations than to be asked about anonymous letters.

'Good lord no, Inspector; here in Twytching? Surely someone's having you on. It sounds too melodramatic for words.'

'No question of that, sir, I'm afraid. Then you haven't had one, and neither did your wife to your knowledge?'

'Certainly not as far as I'm concerned. And I'm as sure as I stand here that if Alison had got one she'd have shown it to me.' He paused almost sentimentally. 'It would have amused her no end, Inspector. She found this rather a dead-end place, you know. She liked to – what's the phrase?

–*épater les bourgeois.* It would have tickled her to think she had done it to such good effect that someone wrote a poison-pen letter to her. It was that sort of thing you were meaning, was it, Inspector? Or was it some attempt at blackmail?'

'As far as we can judge from the others,' Parrish said carefully, 'these are just poison-pen efforts. But the one often shades off into the other, or develops into it, you know. We've no means of knowing whether it did in this case or not.'

'Alison certainly hadn't had any money off me recently to pay blackmailers,' said Mailer with a weary smile. 'Though looking at a collection of gramophone records I've just discovered that I knew nothing about, she would have been wanting money pretty soon. She was a wonderful woman, Inspector, but she never could resist an impulse.'

'And you can think of nothing that she might have been blackmailed about, sir?' asked Parrish. 'Nothing in her past?'

'Good lord no, Inspector. The idea's absurd. Just who has given you this crazy idea?'

'Well, we know that some kind of anonymous letter was delivered here in the last few weeks.'

Arnold Mailer thought for some moments. 'That means old Amos Chipweather told you he'd brought one, I suppose. Well, I won't try to teach you your job, Inspector.' Courteously he let the sentence stand in the air.

'So far as you are concerned, sir, you received no letter?'

'Definitely not, Inspector.'

'And your wife couldn't have opened your mail for you?'

'Absolutely not! What an idea! That sort of thing's not on these days, is it?'

Inspector Parrish, in common with the rest of Twytching, knew of one household where it certainly was on, but he refrained from pressing the matter. As things stood there seemed three possibilities. Either Mailer was lying and had received one; or his wife had opened it without telling him;

or she had received one herself. On the whole the last seemed the most likely, but there was no evidence either way.

At the top of the stairs Parrish had a word with Constable Lockett, who was co-ordinating the police endeavours around and in the house. Lockett was slow, but he had a hunting-dog's thoroughness, and if he knew what he was looking for, he generally found it. The trouble was, Parrish thought, that he had been able to give him so few indications of what he should be looking for.

'There's very little, sir,' said Fred. 'Nothing personal from the lady's side at all. No letters, like – only business things : insurance on her jewels, enquiries about things advertised in the newspapers, and that kind of thing. Only trace of blood anywhere is on the chopping board in the kitchen. Course we'll go into it, but what would it tell us? Bound to chop a bit out of yourself now and then if you're cooking, if *my* wife is anything to go by.'

'Keep it up, Fred,' said Parrish, and went down the stairs and through the hall, nodding to Cressida who was standing by the mantelpiece in the lounge thoughtfully sucking a pen. He closed the front door quietly and set off back to the station.

During his talk with Arnold Mailer the *This is Twytching* team had moved on, and now the over-hygienic-looking American with the fearsome bonhomie was interviewing Mrs Carrington in her front garden. Mrs Carrington was a woman whose only claim to fame was a lethal line in home-made wines. Postmen and milkmen who had been plied with it tended to let their rounds go hang and sleep it off under nearby hedges. Some unsuspecting Seventh Day Adventists had once given a most curious impression of the tenets of their faith after a brief stop-over at Mrs Carrington's. By the enthusiasm with which both interviewer and production team were quaffing it during the recording of the conversation (Harold Thring was holding aloft his glass and doing a silent but spirited imitation of a certain well-known soprano in the first act of *Traviata*) it seemed likely that the recording schedule would be only spasmodically adhered to on this occasion.

'I think I'd like something operatic,' Mrs Carrington was saying as Parrish passed. 'Could I have "Because"?'

It didn't sound like being much of a programme.

'So unless Lockett and his gang find the letter,' Parrish said to Sergeants Feather and Underwood, thinking what a handsome pair they made seated at Sergeant Feather's desk, and how unlucky it was that Sergeant Underwood had the better brain, 'we seem to have come to a bit of a dead-end in that direction.'

'If only we could establish some kind of blackmail evidence,' said Feather slowly. 'It would at least show for certain why she was there at that time of night.'

'Either giving or receiving, you mean?' said Parrish. 'Or perhaps just picking up. It's a fair point, a possibility. But so far there's no more than a shadow of a suggestion of it. And if she was receiving, then from whom? Who has money in Twytching?'

'There's not even a local squire,' said Sergeant Underwood. 'Or a property tycoon with a weekend cottage.'

'There's Jimson,' said Feather. 'If he hasn't got a private income of some sort, then he's certainly living beyond his means.'

'You've got a grudge against him,' said Parrish. 'Did he keep you in after school for not being able to conjugate "amo"? It's a big house for a schoolmaster, but it's no mansion. Still, I suppose it could be worth looking into. Do you know where he banks?'

'Eastern Provincial,' said Stephen promptly. 'We sometimes meet there.'

'Really? And exchange frosty greetings, I suppose? So he did know one of my men was an old boy of his, did he? Cunning little bugger, making it all so hypothetical. Look – that's where Alison Mailer banked too. Do you think you could go along to get the details on that, and try and get him to show you Jimson's recent statements at the same time? I don't know what sort of pressure you could use – threaten to withdraw your princely savings, perhaps.'

'Hardly,' said Stephen. 'But he does have a nasty Alsatian that takes chunks out of people now and then, so he likes to keep on the right side of the law. I'll play it casual, and see how far he'll step out of line.'

As Stephen set a bloodhound expression on his face and went off, Parrish bent over the anonymous letters newly returned from the police labs in Barstowe, feeling he was looking at them for the umpteenth time.

'That's one line of enquiry,' he said, 'and the other is these little beauties. They worry me, Betty.'

It was not often that he used Sergeant Underwood's Christian name. She glowed.

'They puzzle me,' she said. 'There's something about the style – I can't pin it down.'

'Yes. Of course, whoever wrote them would be a bit limited by what he found in the papers, but still there does seem . . .'

The telephone rang, and he took it up.

'Yes . . . yes . . . that's what I guessed. Yes. No, nothing else for the moment. Thanks a lot for your help.'

He replaced the phone. 'That was Broadwich. They've been on to the BWC, as Livermore calls him. Sir Charles Watson. Never heard of Alison Mailer in his life. Says he meets all kinds of people, so he can't swear he's never seen her or met her casually, but he says he's a good memory for names, and she quite definitely wasn't a friend or acquaintance.'

'As you thought, Inspector,' said Sergeant Underwood.

'Exactly. Naïve, these chaps like Livermore. Don't know they're born. Or perhaps he just couldn't be bothered to check, since it was no skin off his nose. Still, it was a neat little idea on her part.'

'Anyway, it certainly worked,' said Betty Underwood,

and then added : 'Perhaps only too well.'

'Yes,' said Parrish thoughtfully. 'You know, I'm puzzled by one thing. Both the Mailers say she had a lot of friends. Now would you have said that was true?'

'Didn't know the woman well enough,' said Sergeant Underwood. 'It's not usually true with women of that type. Would you like me to do a bit of snooping round?'

'Would you, Betty? Neighbours, parent groups from school, Mrs Leaze – all the obvious sources. Find out just who her friends were.'

When she had gone Inspector Parrish sank back into his armchair, pleased to be on his own. He liked Betty Underwood, but it always made him sad that Stephen Feather wasn't a bit brighter, and seemed destined not to go much further in the hierarchy of the Force. He just didn't use his brain – or what was more pathetic, he did use it, and it got him nowhere. As with those letters, for example. He took up one of them again. Somewhere at the back of his mind a theory had been forming. It pleased him that he could pursue it without witnesses in case it fell speedily to the ground, as he feared it might. He was on very unknown territory for him. He took out a magnifying glass, with a strong sense of the ludicrous and of what Stephen would have said had he been there, and peered at some of the phrases on the letter. He went up closer and closer to the typewritten phrases, and muttered to himself : ' "Fornication, adultery and all uncleanliness." '

He reached over to his desk and took up the phone.

When he finally got through, the lady on the switchboard at Broadwich University was rather dubious :

'The Professor of *English* literature. Well, that's Professor Cant. What was it exactly you wanted?'

Inspector Parrish explained.

'Well, you could try him, I suppose,' said the operator with great reluctance. 'He *is* the expert. I'll put you through.'

The extension rang several times before it was answered.

'Yes, what is it, what is it?' said a querulous voice.

Inspector Parrish explained.

'It is most inconvenient,' said Professor Cant. 'I always have to collect my thoughts before my big lecture, otherwise I lose the thread entirely!'

'There are only three or four phrases,' said Inspector Parrish. 'I got on to you because the lady on the switchboard told me you were the Shakespeare expert.'

'How would she know?' said the peppery voice, refusing to be placated. 'And what a vulgar description!'

'Could I just read you the phrases?' wheedled Parrish.

'Oh, very well,' said Professor Cant testily. 'But I never was very good at guessing games.'

'The first phrase that worries me,' said Parrish, 'is "fornication, adultery and all uncleanliness".'

'Good heavens,' said Professor Cant.

'Then there's "masculine whore" and "a whore and a cuckold".'

'The second could be anywhere,' said Professor Cant. 'Shakespeare is full of whores and cuckolds.'

'Then there's "pigs barbecued in your own shit" . . .'

'Really, that's not a very nice thing to read me just after my lunch . . .'

'And "personal screwing machine".'

'Well, the last two aren't Shakespeare, I'm sure of that,' said the voice of Professor Cant. 'The others – well, really I don't know. You could look up Partridge, I suppose – the Shakespeare bawdy man. I haven't actually *read* those plays for years, you understand, not for years. I just lecture on them.'

'I see,' said Parrish. 'Well, I suppose if you don't know, there's nobody there who would, is there?'

'I don't know about that,' said Professor Cant, clutching at a straw. 'Why don't you try a research student? They *have* to read these things, you know, and it will probably be much fresher in their minds than mine. Let me get you switched over to Porson. He's an able young chap, or so he says anyway. Terribly tiring, I know that. I'll get you transferred."

And Professor Cant went off thankfully to his pre-lecture meditation. Porson was much more helpful, and came up with the answers as quick as a flash.

'Yes, that's Shakespeare,' he said. '*Troilus and Cressida*. Probably Thersites. Yes, definitely, but I can't tell you the act or scene. The other's *Measure for Measure* – the whole play's about fornication and adultery and that. It'll probably be in the low comedy scenes somewhere.'

'Splendid,' said Parrish, appreciating the proximity of a university for the first time. 'What about "personal screwing machine"?'

'Well, not Shakespeare, of course,' said the prodigy. 'Modern. It rings a bell. Could it be the young chap – Nick, isn't it? – in *Who's Afraid of Virginia Woolf*?'

'You could be right,' said Parrish, who had seen the film and thanked his lucky stars for his bachelorhood for days afterwards. 'What about "pigs barbecued in your own shit"?'

'Oh yes, that's easy. That's Osborne. *Small Hotel in Amsterdam*. Right at the end. The BADS are doing it, that's how I know. The Broadwich Amateur Dramatic Society. Anything else? Well, glad to have been of help – any time, any time.'

Parrish could picture him putting down the phone, and positively basking in his own cleverness. He reminded him of some of the people on *University Challenge*.

That, so far as it went, was satisfactory. What Parrish couldn't decide was how far it actually went. Not very, he feared, and very probably in the wrong direction at that. The trouble with this case . . . but his thoughts were interrupted by Constable Lockett, who brought him the results of the search of the Mailer home. He put them down on Parrish's desk apologetically, like a dog who knows it has been sent to retrieve a partridge, but has found nothing bigger than a sparrow.

'And if you can make anything much out of that lot,' he said glumly, 'I'll be surprised.'

The notes on the various parts of the house were indeed bare. From them, as from the house itself, one got an un-lived-in feeling. It seemed like a house where someone regularly swept through, removing the evidences of human-ity. Mrs Mailer, of course. Very much the de-humanizing type. No stacks of old magazines in *her* house, no senti-mental treasuries of letters or mementos, no holiday snap-shots or wedding groups. Parrish could guess how Alison would have reacted to the idea of displaying these last items. The Mailers' lives seemed a beautiful bare surface. Only in Arnold Mailer's study and Cressida's little room were there vital signs of occupation, of human life going on : business papers, postcards from acquaintances, files of bills were found in the former; games, books and piles of school exercise books in the latter.

Along with the inventory Lockett had brought along the few scraps of personal correspondence he had managed to lay his hands on in Alison's own parts of the house. They concerned minor insurance business or purchases Alison had made or was contemplating. There was a bill from Harrods, and there were replies from advertisers in *The Times* – one from a firm dealing in villa holidays in Italy, the other from the makers of continental quilts.

'Anything interesting?' asked Sergeant Underwood when she came in later and found him mulling over this hoard and getting little out of it.

'Nothing, nothing at all,' said Parrish. 'I suppose you could say that was in itself interesting. Mrs Mailer was a woman who believed in covering her tracks, it seems.'

'That's my impression,' said Sergeant Underwood.

'Is it? No friends, no girls'-get-together groups?'

'Nothing that I can find,' said Betty Underwood. 'Mrs Jimson said she dropped in if she wanted anything, but that there might be months between each visit. The child-ren played together quite a lot, but obviously the mothers didn't get on, though Mrs Jimson says they never had anything definite like a quarrel. Mrs Mailer had been to one or two parents' evenings at the school when she first arrived, but she lost interest, and anyway the girl's gone on to Barstowe Grammar. She seldom shopped in Twytching, and she antagonized everyone when she did by acting the colonel's lady. So far as I can discover she had no close friends, male or female.'

'That was my impression of the poor creature, I must admit,' said Parrish. 'And I can understand her having few friends, or none at all come to that, because she wasn't a comfortable body to be with, I suspect. But the Mailers were deceived, so presumably she had business that took her somewhere now and then in the evenings. Where did she go? And what I don't cotton on to is this habit of cleaning up behind her, so to speak. It seems almost obsessive. Why?'

'I wouldn't put too much weight on that,' said Betty Underwood. 'It's common enough – just a more elaborate version of not wearing dirty underclothes in case you get run over. And then, if some people see something out of place, their fingers itch till it's put back again.'

'Seems just plain bloody unnatural to me,' said Parrish. 'And it certainly puts a full stop to our enquiries all down the line. Ah – here's Stephen.'

Stephen was looking modestly pleased with himself, though not in any way bursting with illumination.

'There's something here,' he said, 'though I'm damned if I see exactly what it is.'

'Spill the beans,' said Parrish. 'Little Mr Price was friendly, was he?'

'Oh, very,' said Stephen. 'Quite hail-fellow-well-met and what can I do for you? Made no trouble at all about formalities. Well then, first of all the Mailers have separate accounts.'

'That's what I'd imagine,' said Parrish. 'There'd never

be anything in a joint account if she had her own cheque-book.'

'There was never a great deal in Arnold Mailer's account as it was,' said Stephen. 'She was obviously an expensive wife. He's got a good salary coming in, and no need to worry, but still they lived more or less up to their income. Hers was an interesting account, though. Never anything much in it for years, just an allowance put in monthly. Then last summer there starts coming in a series of fairly large cash sums – in hundreds and two hundreds at a time, and three hundred on one occasion. Irregular this, with no rhyme or reason about it. She spent much of it – there are largish cheques to clothes shops, furniture shops, record shops, places like that.'

'Interesting,' said Parrish.

'Very,' said Stephen. 'Seems to me as if blackmail is in the air.'

'And Jimson?' asked Parrish. 'What about him?'

Stephen looked disappointed and less sure of himself.

'Well now, there's an odd account, too. It's always in the black, though never spectacularly so. There seems to be no private fortune, no shares or anything that the bank manager knew about. But good little sums keep going in regularly: fifty, a hundred, two hundred. The manager had never questioned this: he thought it must have come from his writing.'

'Didn't know there was so much in verse drama,' said Parrish. 'You should try your hand at writing it, Stephen.'

'And these sums came in cash, too,' said Feather, ignoring him. 'Doesn't sound like any publisher's payment to me.'

'Hardly,' said Parrish. 'Much too open-handed. And it wouldn't be for his column in the local paper either. I don't imagine he makes much more than seventy-five pee a pop for them. It's not the big time. What about the out-going?'

'Nothing very interesting there,' said Stephen. 'Usual

bills paid, and the rates, and that sort of thing. But he took seventy-five out in cash earlier this month, and there was an unexplained fifty in April – these could be worth looking into. But there's no evidence of his being milked over a long period, or anything like that. It's a big house, and they've three children. Even with these extra sums he doesn't have a lot to spare.'

'I imagine not,' said Parrish vaguely. He always imagined family men to be presented with incessant bills for new school-blazers and water-boots. 'Well, so the picture as I see it is that they both have some sort of unidentified income. Nothing spectacular in either case, but bringing in the sort of tidy sum that makes all the difference between struggling along and managing quite nicely thank-you. What's it all about, do you imagine? Neighbours in crime?'

'There was no correspondence in the dates they put the money in – I checked that,' said Stephen.

'Marvellously co-operative your Mr Price.'

'Oh, he was,' said Stephen. 'Nice as pie. Until . . .'

'What?'

'As I got up to go, he reminded me I was twenty-five quid overdrawn.'

'Never trust the friendliness of bank managers,' said Parrish.

He sat down in his big desk chair, pondering. Stephen Feather never liked him much in that mood. It always meant that he was even more moves ahead of him than usual. Stephen had all the buoyant self-confidence of the young, but he hated to be humiliated in front of Sergeant Underwood.

'You'd agree about blackmail, wouldn't you, sir?' he asked.

Inspector Parrish waved his arms impatiently. 'Oh yes, perhaps – blackmail or something crooked or dubious at least. There's been something going on, certainly. The trouble with this case, though, is that it seems to point in two different directions.'

'Really?' said Stephen. 'At least I should have thought it was clear this Mailer woman was writing letters, terrorizing people, and then making demands on them.'

'It's a possibility,' said Parrish.

'They've stopped since she died.'

'Of course they've stopped,' said Parrish impatiently. Then he seemed to forget Feather, and his slowness. As if talking to himself, but actually addressing himself to Betty Underwood, he said: 'Two different directions. The problem is, are they connected? Or is one a snare and a delusion? In the long run we've got to concentrate on the Mailer woman.'

'Obviously,' said Stephen sourly, 'since she's our corpse.'

'Exactly. And it's there the problem is. No common ground. The family apparently thinks one thing, everyone else another. Someone's lying, probably her. And she's dead, and has left behind not a scrap of personal evidence, nothing to get at the truth of her personality with.' He paused. 'Unless . . .'

'What?' asked Betty Underwood.

'Exercise books,' said Parrish. 'The little girl's always writing. I wonder if it's worth looking at her exercise books.'

CHAPTER XI

A CHILD AMONG YOU
TAKING NOTES

It was early evening by the time Parrish got to the Mailers' again, a May evening full of nip and near-summer. He found Arnold Mailer and Cressida having toasted cheese on the sofa in the sitting-room, and only reluctantly conscious of anyone but themselves. He guessed that informal meals of this kind hadn't been approved of before, and that their meal had the advantage in their eyes of homeliness and near-picnic conditions.

'We're trying to get used to our loneliness, Inspector,' Arnold said, getting up as Parrish came in, and gesturing him unconvincingly to a chair. 'It's so strange to us, having only each other : it seems as though somehow we're having to get to know each other all over again.'

Parrish refused the chair, and made little apologetic noises indicating an unwillingness to interrupt as he awkwardly tried to explain himself and his mission.

'I'm just collecting a few things, sir, just trying to . . . build up a picture, as it were, get an idea of . . . well, what sort of woman Mrs Mailer, er, your wife, that is, was. If you'll excuse me I'll just go upstairs and try to lay my hands on what I want. Naturally I'll give you a receipt for anything I take.'

'Of course you must just take anything you think might be useful,' said Arnold Mailer. Cressida smiled at him her beautiful smile, and as he left to go upstairs they turned back to their meal, quite absorbed in each other.

Parrish returned the few personal letters and papers Alison had left behind to her dressing-table, where they had lain openly in a drawer. The top of the table was littered with make-up and scent. To Parrish's inexperienced eye they seemed to be all of an exclusive and expensive type : they were classically simple bottles, with unobtrusive, enigmatic labels, and they were ranged in military rank, each in its place waiting for its dead user. It was clear that the Margaret Thatcher cool exterior which Alison presented to the world was a surface which had taken her time and money to perfect.

Cressida's room was more lived in, and much more to Parrish's liking. Games and books were stuffed higgledy-piggledy on shelves, and books lay open on spare spaces all around the room, half-read and waiting to be continued with. Cressida seemed to have a catholic taste, and to be at that intermediate stage between childish and adult reading. Since there were also several very old cuddly toys in places of honour on the high shelves it seemed as though the girl's whole childhood was encompassed in the untidy little box of a room.

The exercise books were stacked in a comparatively tidy pile right by the bed. Parrish flicked through several, discarding the maths, the geography and the Latin ones. After looking into them he discarded the French ones too: Cressida would only have started the language recently, and did not seem to his inexpert eye to be far enough advanced to say anything interesting in it. Slipping into his briefcase a collection of English books, and adding some history ones on the off-chance, Parrish crept downstairs again and went quietly out the front door.

The Radio Broadwich team had resuscitated itself by now, and was somewhat blearily proceeding with the business of putting a programme together. It wasn't the sort of job for a home-made hangover, and as Parrish drove past them he had the impression that tempers were frayed. They were all standing by a little van (the inevitable knot of onlookers around them) interviewing Mrs Brewer, who was reaping a just reward for a month of vehicularized shepherd's pies and meat and two veg. Hank was bravely sampling something, without abating a jot of his joviality. The clatter of plates was meant to add verisimilitude, and it didn't seem to be bothering anyone that it was by now nearly six o'clock and all self-respecting pensioners would be tucked up in front of children's television. Parrish had a sinking feeling in his stomach that if Mrs Brewer had a choice of music to be played it was going to be 'If I Can Help Somebody'.

Back at the station, he caught Feather and Underwood in the middle of an intensely serious analysis of the case, including a detailed analysis of the murderer's mind, which Parrish thought distinctly futile until they knew why the murder had been done. He scattered the exercise books on the table, and looked at them.

'It's a long shot,' he said, 'but a damned sight more useful than what you're doing at the moment. The little girl seems to like writing, and at that age you've no great experience outside the home. So my idea is that we ought to get some reference or other that at the very least ought to fill in the background – tell us what sort of a mother this Mrs Mailer was, what sort of things she did with her time, give us some notion of what the home life was like there. With a bit of luck we may even get something more substantial, but I'm not banking on that.'

He paused, shaking his head dubiously. Then he said : 'All right, get reading.'

Parrish himself had carefully kept his fingers on the exercise books that seemed most likely to fill in the picture for him. They were the most recent in date, and were marked 'English Composition'. Two of them were labelled 'Twytching Primary School', and the other 'Barstowe Grammar School'. He took the Twytching ones first, thinking them the more likely to contain local details. He accustomed his eyes to the square, neat, upright writing, not unlike that of some of his constables, and began reading himself into Cressida's childhood.

His first impression was that it was not surprising that Cressida Mailer had passed her eleven-plus (which still existed in the county more than a decade after the all-powerful gentlemen in Whitehall had issued the diktat decreeing its speedy fading from the face of the earth). He suspected that for her age – it must have been about ten at the time – her command of spelling, punctuation, sentence structure and style were well beyond her years, and especially remarkable in an age which seemed to consider such things dispensable frills or pedantic irrelevancies. There was a wonderful flow about her work, as if she could enter into a world of her own and recreate it effortlessly in words. The red pencil of the teacher had had little to do beyond correcting the odd 'independant' for 'independent', the sort of mistake that every self-respecting person makes at that age, and much later.

The next impression was that the girl must have had a very good teacher. He wondered whether it might be little Miss Marriot of the Drama Group and the Amenities people. She was the pink rosebud type in appearance and manner, but Parrish had always suspected her of concealing something energetic and imaginative in her make-up well beyond the power of Twytching to bring to the surface. The exercise book suggested that, whoever it was, she and Cressida had enjoyed a close and fruitful relationship.

Some of the essays were conventional enough. 'My Favourite Animal' was one, and Parrish remembered that there were no dogs or cats in the Mailer home. But there was no repining at this in the essay. Cressida had chosen no run-of-the-mill animal of this sort. She had written on the giraffe – a vivid, impressionistic piece about its movement, its 'long-legged grace', its 'haughty splendour', and how feeble, limited and unadaptable mere humans must appear to 'the lordly, long-necked kings of the forest'. It was a delightful little piece, and the remarks written in a school-mistressy hand underneath showed that it had been highly appreciated.

Other subjects were more imaginative. Towards the end of her last year in the Twytching Primary School the teacher had made the class embark on a series of related stories, in which they created an imaginary country for themselves, and peopled it as they chose. Cressida had come up with a Brontë-like confection which she called Morganaland. It was apparently an undiscovered island in the Pacific, peopled by a number of clans, quarrelsome, jealous and treacherous, not unlike the early Scots. They were ruled over by a Queen, a cold, ambitious, deceitful woman, totally unscrupulous in playing off one clan against another, one admirer against another, equally ruthless in sending this man to his execution, or arranging the sudden knife in the dark for another. It was a remarkable little scenario, running in all to over thirty pages. Its progress was punctuated by marks and remarks from the teacher, and Parrish was pleased to see that she expressed no objection to the raging, romantic bloodthirstiness of it all. Instead she seemed taken by the graphic nature of the writing, the bravura style.

All this was fascinating, but not in the personal way which might have been useful. When he took up the first of the Barstowe Grammar School exercise books Parrish noted an immediate change of tone. The change of school could have done it, and the mystic qualities the English attach to the age eleven. Certainly the tone and feeling of the essays were damped down, in comparison with the earlier ones, and Parrish suspected the change of teacher had not been to her benefit. This new one seemed not to welcome extravagance, perhaps had ridiculed luxuriant verbiage, and so had not been given it. Again, the subjects set for the essays had been decidedly unimaginative, and had evoked a corresponding response. 'The First Week in a New School' was the opening essay in the book, and here Cressida's few linguistic flourishes had been underlined, and 'exaggerated' written in the margin. There was little personal in the piece, beyond the fact that her father had brought her to school on the first day. Later in the term she had been given subjects such as 'A Description of a Building', 'Autumn', and 'For and Against Compulsory Games'. The essays were flat. In January the first piece had been about her Christmas, the inevitable topic. Parrish learned that the Mailers had had duckling à l'orange, with a sorbet to follow, but little more.

The notion that Cressida's teacher had little imagination when it came to thinking up essay topics was reinforced when he found as one of the topics after the Easter break a piece called 'What I Did Over the Easter Holidays'. That was the sort of thing that even Charles Lamb would have flagged over. But as he started reading, his interest was caught.

'Mummy decided,' the essay began, 'that we should do things together this Easter. She said that since I had gone away to school she hardly knew me any more. I was very excited, and wondered what we should do to-gether.'

At last, thought Parrish, at last she is going to give some-thing of herself. How odd that she should have managed to keep it out of her essays all this time.

'First we did a lot of cooking together,' Cressida went on. 'I like cooking, and do it fairly often if I get the chance, but now we tried some very unusual recipes: saltimbocca from Italy, chicken and almonds from China. I tried to imagine as I was cooking the sort of people who would eat them in their own country. Mummy let me do things myself, and gave good advice about the sort of spices to use, and how much to put in. She said the whole art of cooking is in the spices.

Then we went to some films in Barstowe and Broad-wich, including *The Railway Children,* and to the theatre in Norwich, which was *Private Lives* by Noel Coward, which was very funny and entertaining, though the people were a bit silly and I couldn't understand why they got divorced if they were really in love with each other after all.

We went for some long walks too, which was nice of Mummy because I don't think she really likes walking, and has not got the right shoes for it. One day in the afternoon we went nearly to Croxham and walked in the woods there. There were all kinds of wild flowers out, and we saw a squirrel right close up. It looked at us for a long time, with its paw up against its cheek as if it was considering us. Then it flicked its tail and scuttled away. That was a funny walk, because a little bit later we were walking quietly in case we should see any more strange animals or birds when we suddenly heard a little scream and laughter, and I saw a girl get up from behind a bush and start to run away, but a man popped up and grabbed her and they disappeared again. We were very surprised, but we just walked on quietly. I think it must have been a little girl playing with her daddy, but I was too short to see him properly. Anyway, that's what Mummy said it was, but she said it was best not to talk about it.

I like going for really long walks, because there is always something interesting to see and hear.'

Parrish sat back in his desk chair, thinking, digesting this turn. Finally he turned to Sergeants Underwood and Feather, who were deep in parsing and the causes of the French Revolution, and not seeming to get much out of them, and said rather hesitantly: 'Can I read something out to you?'

They both put down their books, and Parrish read haltingly the essay dated April 30th. When he finished there was silence for a minute, and then Stephen Feather said: 'We're on to something.'

Parrish twisted his face into an expression of pain, as he sometimes did when he was thinking, and then said: 'Yes, I think so. But what?'

He threw the exercise book over to them to look at, and there was silence in the room for a bit. Then Stephen said: 'Blackmail, I suppose.' He went on slowly and hesitantly: 'Try it this way: Alison Mailer saw something which she knew could ruin the people involved – or the man, rather. She recognized him; being much taller than the girl she saw more of him than she did. This was fairly recently, so almost immediately she must have started blackmailing him.'

'Being already in the blackmailing business, presumably,'

said Parrish, 'and knowing the ropes.'

'Already? Oh yes, the money in the bank. Yes, I suppose this one's not the only one. And the letters imply there would be others. Then he finds out who it is is milching him, arranges a meeting near the bluebell woods . . .'

'But would she go?' said Sergeant Underwood.

'Well, follows her, then, and kills her.'

'Him, or one of the others,' said Parrish.

'True, him or one of the others,' said Stephen. 'We've obviously got to find out who they might be, if we can. But the point is, he's the one we do know something about.'

'So far, so good,' said Parrish. 'It works out convincingly enough, and Mrs Mailer is the sort who wouldn't think twice about methods if she needed a constant supply of extra money each month. But I see her as the cautious type, not in the least slovenly about detail. The question is, how did he find out who'd got him on the hook?'

'Well, it happens. There could be some agreed hiding-place, somewhere where the money was hidden each time. He waits there, sees her, and then does her in. You know the sort of thing.'

Parrish shook his head dubiously. 'Sounds a bit childish, and not really Alison Mailer. Poste Restante would be easier, and she could be pretty sure there'd be no question of bringing the police in, not in a case of this sort, so it'd be safe enough.'

'Does the way he found out matter terribly at this stage, sir?' said Stephen, who sometimes found Parrish's mind too concerned with details and not really alive to the larger strategy.

'Everything matters,' said Parrish. 'And there is another possibility . . . as to how he found out, I mean.'

Stephen looked at him, puzzled. There was silence in the room for a moment.

'The essay,' said Sergeant Underwood.

'Precisely,' said Parrish. 'I wonder who teaches English to the first-year children at Barstowe Grammar.'

'Well, plenty could,' said Stephen, 'there wasn't any one pers . . . Christ! I wonder if you're right.'

'Who's the headmaster there?' asked Parrish. 'Couldn't you ring him and find out?'

'Smithson. I'll get him,' and Feather darted over to the telephone directories and was flicking through them in a second. Marvellous in a chase, Stephen would be, thought Parrish idly to himself. Pity there hasn't been a chase in Twytching in living memory. In little more than a minute Feather was on to his man.

'Yes, sir, Feather . . . I finished five years ago . . . No reason why you should, sir . . . Just plodding along . . . I suppose you'll have heard of the Mailer case, sir? Well, I'm with the police at Twytching, and we're on the case at the moment . . . yes, very sad, very . . . you know the little girl, do you, sir? . . . Yes, very bright, that was our impression . . . we wondered who her English teacher might be . . . really? That's terribly helpful . . . no, no, nothing serious . . . just a little thing we picked up from her English essay book, and we wondered how she came to write it . . . one checks everything in a case like this, of course – a terrible lot of routine . . . I'm awfully grateful to you, sir, awfully grateful . . . I'll hope to see you at Old Boy's Day . . . Stephen Feather, that's right . . . yes, goodbye, and thanks.'

He put the phone down.

'If he swallowed that explanation of why you wanted to know,' said Parrish, 'he doesn't deserve to teach PT in a mission school in Bangladesh.'

'Who cares about that?' said Stephen. 'I was too excited to think up anything, and he'll know there are things we just can't reveal. The main thing is, we've got it in one.'

'Jimson?'

'Takes IA English. Poor little buggers. And likes little girls, the letter said. She should know. She'd seen him at it. What he didn't show us were the letters asking for money: fifty in April, then seventy-five this month. Going up, and as far as he knew, could go on and on, up and up all the time. Then Cressida wrote this essay.'

'Timothy Jimson,' said Parrish meditatively. 'Not a chap I ever cared for. Wouldn't you agree, Stephen?'

The *This is Twytching* interview with Timothy Jimson was recorded in the front room after he came home from school. He had ordered the room to be cleared of all toys, games, and other childish impedimenta, and had even, miraculously, made a few feints of assistance himself. He had then scattered books around the room – the odd Folio title, the poems of Philip Larkin, and an American blockbuster detailing the ecological crimes of humanity. There was also a recently printed copy of *Troy Weight,* inscribed to Hank Nelson, the intimidatingly wholesome interviewer. Hank himself, and most of the production team, were still looking a little frazzled, especially Harold Thring, who didn't improve with frazzling. Ted Livermore, on the other hand, in spite of bloodshot eyes, had more vivacity about him than at any time since he arrived in Twytching, and seemed from his manner to be distinctly chuffed with himself.

'Then you find a receptive audience in Twytching, do you, Tim?' Hank was saying expansively, microphone in hand, his eye on the slowly turning tape, 'and a good atmosphere for your work as a Writer?'

'Remarkably good,' said Timothy genially, rubbing his hands. 'A really intelligent interest taken, by everyone in the village really, and the sort of peace and quiet that a Writer simply *must have* if he is to develop himself fully.'

Jean Jimson stood ignored in the bay window, and watched her husband unblushingly contradict the opinion he had often expressed to her that the people of Twytching were the closest thing on this earth to a bunch of turnips, and that the last trump itself would have difficulty in arousing in them a spark of intelligent interest or lively anticipation. The thought that anyone was in the room who might remember, and make a connection, did not occur to Timothy. His wife existed, but she did not think. But she watched him quietly as he flowered into ludicrous shapes of conceit under the inept questioning.

'Now, I'd say it was about time we had a musical interlude,' the interviewer was saying, when he was interrupted by Parrish ringing the door-bell.

'Damn,' said Harold shrilly. 'We'll have to do that again. Let them in, whoever it is, but tell them to be quiet as *mouses*, PLEASE !'

Parrish and Feather crept into the hall, like Gilbert and Sullivan constables, and stood by the door, watching, as Harold fussed around the tape recorder, and then said : 'Once more that last bit, and be *quiet*, everyone, *please.*'

Timothy Jimson hadn't turned round, being intent on swapping sophisticated chat with his interviewer, and on giving the appearance of being above noticing who had come to see him in his moment of glory.

'Now, I'd say it was about time we had a musical interlude,' said Hank again. 'Would you like to suggest a piece that we can play for you and for all our listeners back in Twytching, Wisconsin?'

Timothy Jimson allowed a fraction of a second to elapse, as if for thought.

'I'd be most grateful if you could play the finale of Haydn's *Military* – the number one hundred. Beecham, of course.' He smirked.

'Right,' said Ted. 'That's in the can.'

'Right,' shrieked Harold. 'Back to the Lamb. *Careful* with that mike, ducky. It's Swiss, and cost a pretty penny, I can tell you.'

If Timothy Jimson was terrified at the sight of Inspector Parrish and his sergeant, he disguised it well. Across the dissolving chaos of the Radio Broadwich men and their apparatus he looked no more than disconcerted, though there was certainly no smile of welcome, and he threw a particularly suspicious glance in the direction of Feather.

'Oh, Inspector,' he said. 'Does it have to be now?' The

implication of 'you are spoiling my moment of glory' seemed obvious, and he looked in anguish at the retreating figure of Hank, whose back had determination written in every padded inch of it. He had forgotten his copy of *Troy Weight*.

'I'm sorry, sir,' said Parrish. 'These things don't always arrange themselves as we'd like. I think it might be better, sir, if we had our talk down at the station.'

Timothy looked outraged. 'Down at the station? You mean you expect me to come to the *police* station? Absolutely impossible, Inspector, *absolutely* impossible. You can see what sort of a day it's been here, and I've a pile of marking I simply have to get done.'

'On a Friday, sir?' said Parrish. It was Jimson's first indication that he was not dealing with an idiot. 'But I'm afraid I shall have to ask you in any case, sir, marking or no marking. We shall all feel much freer if we're at the station.'

'I'm not going to your damned station in a black Maria like a common criminal,' said Timothy, getting redder and more petulant, as he did when people disagreed with him in staff meetings. 'I told you how careful we teachers have to be. You know our position. What are people going to say when they see me with both of you?'

'I think you'll find, sir,' said Parrish quietly, 'that we can do the whole thing with much less embarrassment to you *and* your family if we go to the station. I'll thank you to put your coat on.'

There was a pause as Timothy looked at the Inspector. He seemed to be girding himself up for a further shrill protest. Then he marched out of the room to the coat-stand in the hall, brushing indignantly past the last of the departing technicians. As he noisily and angrily took down a jacket from the hooks, Harold Thring turned to Inspector Parrish, and whispered, in one of his whispers: 'If you arrest him, I'll *never* forgive you, because we'll have to *scrub* the *whole* interview, and then find someone else to represent culture in this *god*-forsaken little town, and if you think that's easy, you have my job, and I'll join the Force!'

Timothy Jimson marched out of the front door, followed by Sergeant Feather, both of them putting up an unconvincing show of being oblivious of each other. Jean Jimson had come to the sitting-room door, but Timothy had ignored her, though he had seen her. At all moments in their marriage when his ego had received a painful blow, he had preferred not to acknowledge her existence. She went back to the bay window, and watched him open the gate – it stuck as usual – and then get into the car. For once the children round her were quiet, not quite able to take in all that had happened in the last hour, and wondering whether their father had got involved in some sort of radio play. As the car drove away, and she caught a last glimpse of Timothy's wizened form, attempting a pitiful, self-important show of righteous indignation, Jean realized that she didn't want her husband to be arrested, not for anything, and not on any account. Because if he was, it would be terribly difficult to leave him. And suddenly she wanted to leave him more than anything on earth.

CHAPTER XII

FINANCIAL AND SCHOLASTIC

'I'm leaving him to you,' said Inspector Parrish to Stephen Feather, after they had dumped Timothy Jimson, pink and protesting, on an uncomfortable upright chair in Parrish's office.

'To me?' said Stephen, who was not used to being given much responsibility beyond checking driving licences and reprimanding small boys caught stealing apples.

'Yes, take my chair. But don't let it give you ideas beyond your station. Range wide, take in all we know, and when he puts up his defences in one direction, come in sideways. Be as sneaky as you know how – provided you keep on the right side of the conventions.'

'It's very good of you, sir. I'm flattered. But is it wise? You saw for yourself how he looked at me when we went to his house. He'll be wild right from the start.'

'And rattled. That's what I want. He'll be expecting me, and what he gets is one of his ex-pupils. And you needn't be too tactful about that, either. Enrage him, get his hackles up, make the blood go to his head – and then –'

'He lets things out?'

'We'll hope so. It's a chance. Remember we've got less than nothing on him so far, that's why you'll have to swerve and dodge as much as possible. The only possible way of closing in on him is by him giving us an opening. He has no alibi, of course : only vouched for till tennish. But then, neither has anybody else, so though we'll check that road as closely as possible, the best openings are likely to come from the man himself. Here our main advantage is the sort of chap he is.'

'A bit of a shit, you mean?'

'You might put it like that. That pretentious, self-important type is very vulnerable as soon as they're faced by someone who isn't impressed by them.'

'Well, I'll do my best, sir.'

'And I'll get Betty to come in and take notes. She'll see you don't overstep the bounds and get us hauled up before the PCS people.'

'The who, sir?'

'Prevention of Cruelty to Suspects. If they don't exist, Jimson will soon found them, if you go too far.'

And Parrish went off chuckling. Stephen Feather stood in the little corridor, preparing his opening moves, then he squared his shoulders, smiled at Betty Underwood, who had turned up with pencil and pad, and went into Parrish's office.

Parrish himself, wondering if he was being quite fair,

swapped a word with Constable Lockett in the main office, gave him a couple of things to do, and then went off into the night with the air of a man who is going to get himself a drink.

Timothy Jimson's first refuge was dignity and monosyllables. But he soon found he had to depart from the latter, and he made a brief statement to no one in particular. It had all the poignancy of an MP protesting to the House that he has not done what everyone knows he has done, and being garlanded with sympathetic wavings of the order papers.

'I must say at this stage that I protest against the manner and timing of my being brought here. I know nothing whatsoever about my late neighbour or her death, and I particularly resent, after the humiliating fuss made at my home in front of my family and the important visitors there, being handed over to an underling for questioning, without so much as a word of explanation. Either this is a matter of importance, in which case the officer in charge of the case should be conducting this interview, or it is not, in which case the behaviour of both of you at my home was deplorable, and will be given the widest publicity. That is all I wish to say, for the moment.'

And having thus threatened the police with 'Twytching Tattle', he pushed up his little chin, gazed into the middistance, and pursed his lips in silent disapproval of all around him. He had thought of adding that he wished to call his solicitor, but then the thought of the cost and the calls on his purse in the past few weeks deterred him, and he decided to use that line only as a last resort.

'Mr Jimson, do you remember what you did during the last Easter vacation?' began Stephen Feather.

'I remember a great many things I did in the last Easter vacation,' said Timothy. 'Be more specific.' He almost added 'boy'.

But being more specific was the problem.

'Were you ever, for example, in the vicinity of Croxham woods during that period?'

'Croxham woods? I don't know. Possibly. I may have taken the family there for a picnic.'

'You *may* have done,' said Stephen, struggling to rid himself of a feeling that he was a not very bright 1C schoolboy, unable to define what an adjectival clause was.

'Yes, I may have done,' said Timothy, simulating an easy contempt.

'Easter is – what? – five weeks or so away, and yet you don't remember?'

'As a family man, with a full-time job and a host of writing commitments, my life is far too full to remember precise dates and exact details,' said Timothy.

'Do you frequently take your family on picnics?'

'Now and then, now and then,' said Timothy, who almost never did. 'Let's cut this short and say that as far as I remember we have *not* had any picnics in Croxham woods for the past year. Now, does that satisfy you?'

'It makes things clearer, yes,' said Stephen, looking down at some wholly imaginary notes to give himself time. 'Now, forgetting your family for the moment, sir, is there anything else that could have taken you to Croxham woods?'

Timothy paused before saying, 'A writer frequently has need for periods of peace and quiet – away from the family.'

'But you don't recall having been there recently?'

'No. Almost certainly not.'

Stephen adopted Parrish's suggestion of an almost complete change of tack.

'Mr Jimson, may I ask you about your financial affairs?'

'No.'

'Do you own your house?'

There was a long pause during which Timothy Jimson

seemed to be weighing the consequences of not answering at all. Finally he said: 'Yes . . . well, it's on a long mortgage.'

'It's a fairly large house.'

'I have a family, as you will have observed.'

'The payments on it must be high.'

'You may assume the payments to be what you will. I do not see what they can have to do with the death of – '

'Do you have any other source of income, apart from teaching?' asked Stephen, feeling he was getting into his stride now. Certainly Timothy seemed thoroughly disconcerted, for the first time in the interview. There was a pause before he replied.

'I have my writing,' he said at last.

'Your column in the *Barstowe Gazette*?'

'For example.'

'Does that bring you in much?'

'No, it does not. Two pounds fifty a week.' Timothy banged the desk with a dramatic gesture that sent pens and ink-bottles leaping into the air. 'I do not see where this is leading.'

'Do you have any private fortune of your own, sir?' said Stephen calmly, beginning to enjoy himself.

'No, none.'

'And yet you manage to maintain your house and a car on a schoolmaster's salary?'

'Yes.'

'May I ask how?'

'Strict economy and a modicum of common sense,' said Timothy, and again pursed his lips into silence.

'Your bank account shows – '

'My WHAT?'

'Your bank account shows that over the past year or more you have been putting in – '

'It is totally illegal to examine the bank account of any citizen. A special warrant is needed, and application has to be – '

'— putting in what amounts to a regular income in addition to your monthly salary from the County. Fairly regular sums of fifty, a hundred and even more have been paid in. Now, sir, would you like to tell me —'

'I would NOT.'

'— what these were for?'

'NO.'

'Are they, for example, income from your writing?'

Silence.

For the moment Twytching's Torquemada seemed to have reached an impasse in his conduct of the questioning.

When Parrish collected his pint of best bitter from the bar of the saloon at the Lamb, he sensed an Atmosphere. The lowering features of Tom Billington resembled nothing so much as cloud on Table Mountain. However, nobody seemed aware of it in the snug corner by the window where Ted and Harold had ensconced themselves, looking their last on all things Twytching. Ted was in high good humour, making 'in' jokes about the programme which only Harold could understand, and Harold's tetchy, dehydrated condition of earlier in the evening had yielded to the mollifying influence of three gins and tonic. Watched by the locals (who now the programme was in the bag seemed more willing to reveal their opinion that this was an odd pair and no mistake) Ted and Harold were relaxing after the completion of a job well (in their opinion) done.

Parrish lapped up the froth from the top of his glass and went towards them. Harold waved excitedly and shrilled a welcome.

'Lovely!' he said. 'You know, I've suddenly realized what we've been missing on the programme. It's the Law. We ought to have had the Law. But you're all so *discreet*, so *anonymous*, so "don't mention us by name". But how on earth can the lovely people of Twytching, Wis., learn to love their twin town without hearing from its typical English bobby?'

Parrish spread himself into a chair, and expanded into geniality with the first good draught of beer.

'And what was it you were wanting to ask us, then, Inspector?' said Ted Livermore.

'Well, now,' said Parrish, 'you've got it in one.'

'Ah, and there's me thinkin' it was the pleasure of me company he wanted,' said Harold in a mock-Irish accent and twisting the ends of his mouth down into a tragic droop.

'It's no more than a few loose ends, really,' said Parrish. 'We've established that Mrs Mailer was no friend of your Big White Chief, by the way, so I'm afraid she put it over you there, sir.'

'Clever little dodge,' said Ted without rancour. 'Pity she got done in – we could have done with her this week.'

'Barrel-scraping, that's what we've been doing,' said Harold, in a whisper which by morning was all over Twytching.

'Now, the day she came to see you – am I right in thinking that was the day Mr Thring came to Twytching, sir?'

'That's it, Inspector,' said Ted. 'He came as the advance party, as it were.'

'Bearing the flag, or possibly carrying the can,' said Harold.

'Do you remember the exact date, sir?'

'I'll look in my diary,' said Harold, leaning down and diving into the green shoulder-bag on the floor beside him. 'Here it is! One should always have something outrageous to read on the train.'

'*Importance of Being Earnest,*' said Parrish.

'Real little Lord Peter, aren't we?' said Harold, flicking through the pages. 'Goodness, how time flies! Seems like only yesterday Jocelyn and I said our farewells, and here it is – January! That's a really poetic bit I wrote then, Inspector – you'll have to let me read it to you some time. Now where were we? Late March – no, early April. Here we are: April 10th. When I die April 10th will be engraved on my heart.' He fluttered his eyelashes in the direction of Tom Billington, who was not in the least responsive.

'Could you tell me what you did on that day, sir?' asked Parrish.

'I love all these "sirs",' said Harold. 'Well, let's see. I ate mountains of home-made scones and special country-recipe fudge. Let me not think of it, O Lord, or I shall be made mad! Frankly I don't care if I never touch another . . . oh, well, yes – let's see: I talked to lots of the ladies – Mrs Carrington, Mrs Buller, the meals-on-wheels lady – Mrs Brewer, isn't it? Then there was that Val Rice – I was watching her technique, I can tell you. And the cat lady, and the handicrafts lady. Oh, practically the whole town, Inspector, was laid before my conquering feet. And then, of course, that was the day I had my dramatic confrontation with Medusa.'

'With who, sir?'

'Deborah Withens. Doesn't it sound too Emily Brontë?'

'What exactly did you talk about, sir?'

Harold Thring gave a highly coloured account, making it sound rather like one of the more stirring passages of *Il Trovatore*. Parrish de-coloured it by several shades, and felt he probably had the rough idea. After all, Deborah Withens was fairly Verdian.

'And so you had to make it clear to her, did you, sir, that she would not be on the programme?'

'Of *course*, Inspector. Ted could tell by a glance at the letter she wouldn't be suitable, couldn't you, my sweet? Anyway, the Yanks don't want to hear interviews with Chairmen and Mayors and things – it would make us sound like *Toytown*! Mr Growser, sir!' concluded Harold, with a spirited imitation of Larry the Lamb.

'And you also got across the idea, did you, that she wouldn't have a say as to who was and was not on the programme?'

'Not on your life, she wouldn't,' said Harold. 'The *idea*!'

'And you got out alive, sir?' asked Parrish, downing the last of his pint.

'We have our defences, Inspector,' said Harold, with a brave-pathetic smile. 'We've developed them over the years.'

'One thing before you go, Inspector,' said Ted Livermore. 'Now this Timothy Jimson . . .'

'Yes, sir?'

'Was that just a routine matter you took him in for?'

'I can't discuss that, sir, obviously. Shall we just say that he is still helping the police with their enquiries?'

'Would you say there was any question of our – shall we say, finding it best not to use the interview with him?'

'That I couldn't say, sir,' said Parrish. 'But I suppose in these cases you always find it advisable to have an interview in hand, just in case, don't you?'

'Oh NOOO!' shrieked Harold, sending several scalps in the bar tingling with horror in the conviction that the Twytching gytrash was on the trail. 'Not more fairy cakes, I couldn't stand it! Not another glass of parsnip Riesling.'

'Thank Heavens we've still got Hank,' said Ted, looking towards the other end of the bar, where the enormous figure of Hank was soaking up the sheer Englishness of it all, and being fed beer and smut by the locals.

'I insist, I *insist* it's either the cat lady or the flower-arranger,' said Harold. 'Which shall it be?'

'You might say flower-arranging was cultural, mightn't you?' said Ted.

Timothy Jimson watched with distaste written all over his face as Sergeant Feather drew from a drawer in front of him a Barstowe Grammar School exercise book. Timothy had not gone into schoolmastering from a sense of vocation, nor had he developed one over the years. He had taken it up because he had failed to penetrate those bastions of privilege the Foreign Office, the BBC and *The Guardian,* and because a routine muddle at the British Council had left him without a job just when he had been expecting to go spreading D. H. Lawrence and Peter Maxwell Davies among the remote tribes of the Sudan. It is easier to go into school-teaching than to get out of it, and over the years nobody from any of these bastions of privilege, nor indeed anybody from the *Mirror* or the *Sun,* had been so struck by his literary endeavours as to offer him a means of escape. Over those years he had developed a contempt for his pupils, a protective shell of sarcasm against their brutalities, and several techniques for minimizing the cruel workload. He never liked being reminded that he was a teacher, and he certainly did not relish discussing any aspect of his job with a jumped-up mediocrity whom he had once made a feint of teaching.

'Do you recognize this?' asked Stephen.

'An exercise book,' said Timothy.

'The particular essay,' said Stephen, tapping his finger on the page. 'Do you recognize that?'

Timothy cursorily read down the first page. 'Probably one of my kid's efforts,' he said. 'Probably first or second year.'

'If you'd just read to the end, sir,' said Feather.

Timothy continued over the page, and read to the end, betraying no great emotion, though his breathing was very short.

'Odd little piece,' he said.

'You've read it before,' said Stephen.

'Maybe.'

'You've put a mark at the bottom.'

'Oh, for Christ's sake,' said Timothy violently. 'One doesn't actually *read* all this damned stuff. You don't imagine that I spend all my time on the vapourings of these semi-literate morons, do you? I've got five different classes for English, and they all write an essay a week. It'd drive me to the bin to read all that rubbish.'

There was a pause while Stephen Feather wondered whether teachers' reports were such a good substitute for exams after all. When he thought his contempt for Timothy Jimson's methods had been made obvious enough, he said quietly : 'Actually, we thought Cressida Mailer was probably an exceptionally bright child.'

'Oh, is it Cressida?' said Timothy off-handedly. 'She plays with our lot now and then. I suppose she's not a bad prospect, as kids go these days.'

Timothy Jimson was one of those teachers who never gave high marks, and never admitted that a pupil might be bright. Bright pupils were a threat to his mediocrity.

'So you don't recall reading the essay before, then, sir,' said Stephen, 'even though you put a mark on it.'

'No, I don't. I may have skimmed through it. These pieces are all the same.'

'Hardly, in this case, sir. You do see the implications of what Miss Mailer wrote, don't you?'

At last a flush, of anger perhaps, spread over Timothy Jimson's cheek, and robbed him of all semblance of calm.

'Yes, I do see the implications, and I *do* see what you're getting at, and of all the ham-fisted attempts at detection – '

'The connection with the anonymous letter you received was obviously something we had to follow up.'

'There is no connection.'

'You have never been to Croxham woods with anyone other than your family, then, sir? Never with anyone from Barstowe Grammar – one of your girl pupils, for example?'

'I wouldn't be seen DEAD with one of those tittering, snotty-nosed, gym-slipped excrescences,' yelled Timothy. 'It's all someone's dirty-minded fantasy, as you well know.'

'Those sums you've taken out of your account recently,' said Stephen, with an adroit change of gear that left Timothy in mid-splutter. 'What were they for?'

'I'm always writing cheques,' said Timothy. 'Who isn't?'

'This was a fifty in April, and a seventy-five a week ago. They were in cash, and were in addition to your usual weekly sums. What were they for, Mr Jimson?'

'My God,' said Timothy. 'And they talk about the citizen's rights to privacy, and we are supposed to be protected against noise and pollution and computers storing personal data, and snoopers from the Social Security, and it turns out that all the damned police have to do is go along to your bank, and the manager says "Come in and look at the accounts. Take any you please! Fascinating reading!" My God, the editor of *The Times* is going to hear about this, I can tell you.'

Stephen had an uneasy feeling that he might have been a bit too open about what he knew about Jimson's bank account. It occurred to him that a hardly-worth-considering overdraft in the region of twenty-five pounds might find itself called in sooner than he had expected. But he kept his cool admirably, and merely said : 'The sums were fifty pounds in April and seventy-five earlier this month.'

There was silence while Timothy digested his eloquence, and then he said with a feeble show of defiance which showed he knew that the matter was not going to be allowed to rest there : 'They were taken out to meet personal expenses.'

'That doesn't explain,' said Stephen, 'why your expenses were so high in April and May.'

There was a long pause, and finally Timothy made the sort of superhuman effort a climber makes to maintain a precarious finger-hold on the rock-face.

'They were paid to a printer in Colchester,' he said.

It was far from what Stephen had been expecting.

'Indeed, sir? For what?'

'To print copies of my play. *Troy Weight,* you know. I . . . er . . . had it printed at my own expense.'

Timothy Jimson couldn't have looked more embarrassed

if he had just admitted to playing sex-games with little girls.

Parrish collected the notes and reports waiting for him in the outer office, and looked at the clock. It was nearly ten. He looked towards Constable Lockett, and nodded in the direction of his own office. 'Are they still there?'

'Yessir. Seems to be taking them quite a time.'

'Perhaps he'd better stop the night. We could give him the choice between that and going home with a guard on his house. I expect he'd see the point.'

'Maybe,' said Constable Lockett, 'though he doesn't seem to be a very reasonable body.'

'He's got a brain when he cares to use it,' said Parrish. 'It's just that his picture of himself keeps getting in the way.'

'Could I ring the little wife, perhaps, and tell her not to worry?' said the soft-hearted Constable Lockett. 'She's a sensible body, but she must be wondering.'

'Ay, do that.' Parrish mused a moment. 'Doesn't it make you wonder sometimes how two people actually manage to see enough in each other to get themselves married? You look at peop –'

But he was interrupted by an obvious case in point. A hesitant cough from the door told them they were not alone, and a moment later the inconsiderable figure of Ernest Withens slid into view, looking as usual as if his existence was a thing he would not like to be held responsible for. On this occasion his natural tendency towards self-oblitera-tion was augmented by a particularly painful hesitancy.

'Er, Inspector, er . . . do you think . . . I know you must be busy . . . but just a *short* moment . . . I don't think I'd be troubling you unnecessarily . . . if you *could* manage it . . .' He faded to a halt.

'Of course, sir, naturally. I'm afraid my office is in use at the moment. Would you mind coming in here, Mr Withens?'

He led the way to a tiny office, hardly more than a box,

which Sergeant Underwood used when she was reprimanding erring school-children or shop-lifting pensioners. He nodded Ernest Withens to another of the hard, upright chairs, a replica of the one in which Timothy Jimson was at that moment squirming, and then sat down himself behind the desk.

'Deborah doesn't know I'm here,' said Mr Withens, as if assuring Parrish that they were safe from surprise attack. 'She thinks I'm at a meeting of Drains and Sewage.'

'Really, sir?' said Parrish. 'Well, perhaps we could come to what it was you wanted to see me about.'

'It's said, Inspector,' said Ernest, suddenly losing confidence again, 'that you're interested in these . . . er . . . anonymous letters that have been . . . er . . . going around.'

'That's right, sir.'

Words seemed to fail the Chairman at this point, and instead he dived dramatically into his bag, and drew from it a paperback book, which he flourished feebly towards the Inspector.

'Inspector, last night I found *this*.' It was a paperback copy of the Report of the Longford Commission on Pornography. 'I happened to take it from the shelves last night, while Deborah was out,' said Mr Withens. 'I often do, you know. It has some most extraordinary things in it. But now – look at page 97. And page 453.'

Parrish turned as directed. On those pages words had been cut out with a razor-blade. From his memory of the letters he guessed them to have been in one case 'male brothel' and in the other something like 'sexual relationships'. It had been done very neatly, whatever one might think of the decision not to throw away the book afterwards.

'I thought I ought to show you,' said Ernest, now almost puppyish in his eagerness.

'If I were you, sir,' said Parrish, closing the book and handing it back to him over the desk, 'I should put this back on the shelf where you got it from.'

Mr Withens's disappointment was pitiful to behold. His face fell, like a silent film comedian's.

'You do understand what this means, don't you?' he said, almost forcefully. 'Do you mean to say you're not going to do anything about it?'

'I didn't say that, sir,' said Parrish. 'But you've not told me anything I didn't know already. I've just got reports from the CID confirming my guess. No, no – I don't mean that I'm not going to do anything about it.'

'Aaaah,' said Ernest, leaning back in his chair.

'I'm merely suggesting it would be much better in every way if you yourself were not involved.'

This agitated Ernest beyond anything. 'Me, involved, Inspector? Of course I can't be involved. I imagined that would be understood.'

'That's why I suggest you put this back on the bookshelf where you got it from,' said Parrish. 'Where would that be, by the way?'

'Second shelf of the case nearest the window,' said Withens. 'You will be coming to see Deborah, then, will you?'

'First thing tomorow morning,' said Parrish. 'Best to chivvy the breakfast along a little, if you can, sir. But don't on any account alarm Mrs Withens before I come.'

'No, no, on no acount. Quite, absolutely,' bumbled Ernest, clearly working around to another difficult point. 'I suppose you will be forced to arrest her, won't you, Inspector?'

It was quite impossible for Mr Withens to keep the wheedle out of his voice, or the look of excited expectation out of his eyes.

'That I can't say, sir. That's not something we could ever discuss with the general public. I think you can rest assured, sir,' said Parrish, his small vein of malice getting the better of him again, 'that in this case I shall be no harsher than I am forced to be.'

'Oh, quite, Inspector, quite,' said Ernest, deeply disappointed, and getting up to go. 'But of course I expect no favours. None at all. It has always been Deborah's own conviction that people in positions of trust can expect no mercy shown them if they betray that trust. She has often expressed that idea very forcibly. Very often indeed. She'll be waiting for her Ovaltine,' he added, as if a bell had rung in his mind. 'I shall be at the Town Hall tomorrow morning, I'm afraid, Inspector, but I'm sure I can trust you to do your duty without fear or favour. Without fear or favour.'

And Ernest Withens vaporized himself into the night.

CHAPTER XIII

THE LETTER KILLETH

It was a few minutes after nine when Parrish pulled up outside Glencoe, the Withens residence, that Saturday morning. Breakfast had been cooked and served with alacrity, and Deborah Withens (who seemed to the expert eye to have mellowed fractionally over the past week) gave a measured word of appreciation to her husband. Who looked modestly into the pattern of the carpet, and prayed that Deborah would not see the faint sparkle of anticipation in his eye.

Parrish got out of the car, told Constable French, his driver, that he was likely to have a long wait, and went to the wrought-iron monstrosity which served Twytching's Elysée as a gate. He paused as if appalled by his own daring, but he was put in a suitably hostile frame of mind by seeing the regulated, chivvied design of the front garden : daffodils, tulips and gladioli were planted in rows and geometrical clumps, and one had an image of Dame Nature standing over them with a whip, waiting to chastize anything that stepped out of line. Parrish pushed his way through the gate, and rang the front-door bell.

Deborah Withens was undoubtedly in a good mood that Saturday morning. The eggs had been scrambled to that melting consistency she preferred, and the toast had been soft, warm and buttery. Life presented few pleasures to one so worn down by public duties and moral responsibilities, but when it did vouchsafe her one or two, she felt it her duty marginally to unfreeze. Then again the Inspector, once a favourite, had languished in her displeasure for very nearly two months, ever since that deplorable occasion in March when he had more or less suggested that she neglect her bounden moral duty. Seeing him approach up her path from behind the curtain of her sitting-room it seemed to Mrs Withens time to let the bounty of forgiveness shine from her countenance. Thus, when she opened the door to him she let it beam. Temperately.

'Ah, Inspector,' she said, reminding Parrish irresistibly of the Chief Constable of the County, a heavy gentleman of the old school. 'Come to report? Do come into the sitting-room.'

She led the way through the musty hall, with the little tables placed to incommode, and the sneaky legs, poised to trip. She seated him in the place of honour on one side of the drawing-room hearth, drew the heavy curtains to let in a moderate ration of morning sunlight, and sat down on the other side of the fireplace, her hands intertwined genteely in each other, her face set in an expression of polite interest, ready to receive her loyal subordinate's report.

'I shall be most interested, Inspector Parrish, to hear the results of your endeavours so far,' she said.

Well, if that's how you want it, thought Parrish, that's how I'll give it to you.

'I think it may be, ma'am,' he began, 'that this business goes back a long way. As you'll know, most things in a little place like this *do* go back a long way. But perhaps we could start most conveniently with the news that the

Radio Broadwich people proposed to come and record a documentary about Twytching.'

Radio Broadwich. Deborah Withens felt a pang of regret, so sharp as almost to amount to self-criticism; she should never have let out her feelings on that subject so excessively to Parrish on that day in March. But she merely said: 'What a memorable day! As I said to Ernest at the time, it was an opportunity and a challenge!'

'Very well put indeed, ma'am,' said Parrish. 'Now what happened some time after that, though I didn't know it at the time, and few did, was that a series of letters was sent: the first that we know of was in the middle of April, the last at the beginning of this week. They were anonymous letters, in a way you might call them threatening letters, and they went to a number of different people in the village: young Mrs Rice –' (Mrs Withens bridled) – 'the vicar, Tom Billington, one of the Mailers, and so on. By now I expect this is common knowledge around Twytching.'

'I had heard of it, of course,' said Mrs Withens dubiously, 'but I naturally hadn't connected it in my mind with the death of that unfortunate creature.'

'No? But connections there always are, you know, in a town this size. Now, with a spate of poison-pen letters you've very little to go on as a rule. With a clever writer you've little or no chance of getting them.' Mrs Withens's shoulders seemed to unbrace themselves a notch or two. 'What had one to go on here? The addresses were mostly cut from the telephone directory. Anyone can get hold of one. In the letters themselves, most of the words were cut from newspapers, with the *Daily Telegraph* predominating. Well, the *Telegraph* is a popular paper in a village of this sort.'

'I'm surprised but gratified to hear it, Inspector,' said Mrs Withens.

'So all we had that really might give us a lead were a few typewritten phrases here and there, and some words that were cut from paperback books rather than newspapers. Nothing much, but they presented a slender chance of narrowing the field down.'

'Fascinating!' said Deborah Withens perfunctorily.

'But before one could start being at all specific, one had to ask oneself: "What sort of mind is at work here?" and "Why is this being done?" Often the answer to the last question is "sheer nastiness", but I didn't think it was here. As to the sort of mind at work, well, it seemed on the surface to be a peculiarly unpleasant one. One expects some pretty nasty accusations and insinuations, but the language here, ma'am, was of a particularly crude and violent type, and some of the things said about one or two of the people were sheer guttersnipe gossip.'

Mrs Withens faintly nodded her head, as if to say 'I am not unacquainted with such things, alas.'

'But something about the style of the letters suggested to me something other than the usual semi-literate mind you expect in these cases. Now we come to the *purpose* of these letters. Here there were various possibilities to consider. Blackmail was one. Nobody showed us any letter actually demanding money, but that was to be expected. Demands for money sometimes *do* follow a "softening-up" letter of the sort we did get shown.'

Parrish had relaxed considerably, had slid down in his chair, and now he contemplated the appalling light-fitting as he warmed to his subject.

'People think of blackmail in terms of extortion of large sums of money over a period, the sums often getting larger and larger. In fact, it doesn't always work out like that. Blackmailers are often content with small regular sums, the sort of sum that makes the difference between scraping a living and jogging along very nicely. People will do blackmail for the hire of a colour television or a washing-machine. And that's the most difficult sort of blackmail case to crack.'

Mrs Withens had by now also relaxed, and was once again doing her impersonation of the Chief Constable receiving his Inspector's report with kindly interest.

'An appalling crime,' she said without much feeling; 'appalling to contemplate.'

'But again,' went on Parrish, 'I didn't think this case fitted into that sort of pattern. For a start, many of the offences named in the letters were quite simply not of the kind to be susceptible to blackmail. Then there were so many different people written to, and some of them were highly unlikely to pay blackmail money for one reason or another : Mrs Rice, for example, or the vicar. And the fact was that what the letters chiefly seemed to want to ensure was that the recipients kept themselves quiet, avoided publicity, didn't "make an exhibition of themselves", as the saying is.'

'Strange,' said Mrs Withens, with a slight flutter in her voice.

'Isn't it? Now, it occurred to me, Mrs Withens, that the language of these letters was odd. That's not unusual in this sort of communication. But these seemed odd in a peculiar way, and I read some of the phrases to a bright young chappie at Broadwich University. Now these phrases all came from plays, and do you know what? All these phrases were typewritten ones, pasted on to the paper from photocopies, not from originals. Now that gave one to think.'

'Naturally,' said Mrs Withens, seeming to get a grip on herself with difficulty.

'And the other thing one noticed was that these were all cut out in an odd way – they went in at the top, so to speak – and I began to wonder whether in the original they hadn't had quotation marks around them. Stranger still. Where might one find strong, one might say obscene phrases from plays, typed out in quotation marks?'

Mrs Withens let the question hang in the musty air of her sitting-room, and Parrish decided to come straight in for the kill.

'My answer was, in letters to the BBC and similar organizations, complaining about the language in their programmes. And the fact that these were photocopies suggested that the complaints might have been channelled through one of the recognized "watch-dog" groups, who had sent copies of their letters to the original "monitor" or complainer.'

By this point Mrs Withens was forced to make a stand. 'Really, Inspector, I find this fanciful in the extreme, a quite extraordinary line of thought. As you may know, I have been involved with these bodies for some years, and they are composed of the most public-spirited citizens, all of them performing a most valuable public service.'

'We've made an initial check at the offices of the League for the Preservation of Decent Standards in Radio and Television,' said Parrish, producing that mouthful with a flourish, 'and as far as we can see the machine which typed the phrases was one of theirs, an Olivetti Lettera 36.'

'As far as you can see,' throbbed Mrs Withens scornfully.

'We'll be quite definite in a matter of hours. We have also checked the League's correspondence files. All the phrases mentioned were used in letters of protest to the BBC, duplicates of which were sent to you, the original complainant. The phrases came from plays by John Osborne, Edward Albee and William Shakespeare, all performed on television in the last eighteen months.'

There was a long silence in the room, and the morning spring sunlight seemed to tremble near the bay window, wondering whether this was a propitious moment to make a bolder entrance.

'I see now, Inspector,' said Deborah Withens at last, 'the full extent of your fantastic notion. You have come here not to report but to accuse me.' Her mouth twisted convulsively, and her piggy eyes darted murderous glances of outrage and frustrated power-lust. 'Your accusations are ludicrous, based on pure conjecture and the flimsiest of evidence. I defy you to prove them in a court of law!'

'So far, ma'am, the evidence is not quite conclusive, I agree,' said Parrish. 'But I think I can make it more so. One or two phrases were taken from a paperback book.'

He walked towards the window and the sun. 'I think I could lay my hand on the book.'

He darted out a right hand, and took from the shelves Mrs Withens's copy of the Longford report. He brought it to her, and very deliberately opened it at page 97. He let the mutilated page dangle in front of her eyes.

There was a long, long silence in the drawing-room of Glencoe.

Timothy Jimson had had a far from comfortable night at the Twytching police station, and was looking well below his best. A half-hearted growth of stubble disfigured his chin, and indignation struggled with bleariness in his reddened eyes. It didn't make him feel any better to see Sergeant Feather spruce and well-groomed, and obviously prepared to go over and over the same ground as last night until he got the answers he wanted. Nor did it make him feel any better to think that Sergeant Feather was a rather stupid young man who, once he had made up his mind, would probably only accept answers that tallied with his conclusions.

'Then you deny that there were any further letters after the one you showed us?' Stephen asked patiently for the third time.

'I deny it absolutely. And I also deny that there was any attempt to blackmail me.'

'You had no connection, then, with Mrs Mailer, other than that of being next-door neighbours?'

'None whatsoever.'

'And yet you and she were both on the committee of the – ' here Stephen consulted his notes – 'Amenities Group.'

'Yes. But the committee didn't meet.'

'I see, sir. Was there any reason for this?'

'There didn't seem to be any public interest. I sent her notification of the meeting last Monday.'

'But she didn't come.'

'No, she sent apologies, and said she was busy.'

'Busy getting herself murdered, as it turned out.'

'I don't think that a very clever remark.'

'Well, now, sir, while we're waiting to hear from the police in Colchester about the printing of – what was it called – *Troy Weight,* that's right, I think we'd better clear up the business of those sums of money that have been coming into your account.'

Timothy stirred in his seat with extreme irritation. 'They have no connection with anything you're interested in. Even you haven't been able to suggest any possible link. I decline to answer your question.'

'Well, now, sir, we have to follow up many things that seem to have no connection with the main topic of interest. Since the suggestion of blackmail has been made, you must see that it would be as well to clear up every unexplained sum.'

'Could you make up your mind whether you regard me as the blackmailer or the victim,' said Timothy, with pardonable irritation.

'Either, sir, either,' said Stephen Feather blandly. 'Now if you would clear up that matter we could all go home.'

'Don't talk to me like a child,' said Timothy pettishly.

'It's up to you, sir. But I doubt if anyone in Twytching has registered that you're at the police station. We could let you out by the back way as soon as we heard from Colchester, and nobody would be any the wiser. On the other hand, if we are forced to keep you all weekend, it's bound to get around the village.'

Timothy looked at him viciously. 'You're threatening me.'

'Now, sir, with your concern for using words with their precise meaning, I'm sure you must realize I'm doing nothing of the kind,' said Stephen, revelling in having retained that much of Timothy's English classes. 'I'm merely presenting you with the alternatives.'

'That money was earned. Perfectly legitimately.'

'Exactly, sir. All the more reason for telling us.'

'I earned it by my writing.'

'Really, sir? Could you tell me which of your works it was that brought in those kinds of sum?'

There was a threatening pause while Timothy considered his position.

'If word of this ever gets out,' he said, 'I'll sue you.'

'It never will, sir.'

There was another loaded pause. 'I earned it by ghost-writing.'

'Ghost-writing?' said Stephen, astonished. For him the phrase only conjured up the sort of communication with lost loved ones that the vicar claimed to achieve.

'Yes. For Rosaline Macrae. She's getting old and past it, but she still sells like hot cakes all over the world. I give her the manuscript when it's finished, and she pays me cash. That way it's kept between her and me.'

'Rosaline Macrae, sir? Should I have heard of her?'

'She's a –' Timothy Jimson could hardly get it out – 'romantic novelist. Sheer escapist stuff, you know: stable-girl marries Lord of the Manor, hospital romances. She writes the most terrible trash.'

'You mean you write it for her, sir?'

'That's right,' said Timothy Jimson, glaring vindictively at his ex-pupil.

The silence in the drawing-room of Glencoe had indeed been prolonged. Parrish had dropped the odd question into it, but Deborah Withens had merely drawn herself up, and sat silent, staring and immobile, like a Medusa who had inadvertently turned herself to stone.

Finally Parrish decided that if they were not to sit there all day, he would have to do some talking.

'Let's recap a little, then, ma'am,' he said. 'If we can get the whole sequence of events into some sort of perspective, perhaps the whole thing will be easier for us both. Now then, in March you get a letter telling you that the Radio Broadwich people would be coming to Twytching.

Immediately you start planning (against my advice, be it said) the sort of face the village should present to the Americans, and who should be allowed to be on the programme. On April 10th you had a visit from little Mr Thring, the deputy producer, in which he made it clear to you that you would neither be on the programme yourself, as you had assumed, nor be consulted as to who would be. This was a considerable blow to your pride.'

Mrs Withens still sat, like a stalagmite that is getting icy accretions minute by minute.

'The only way you can maintain your reputation in the town is by pretending that the production team has fallen in with your wishes, or at any rate by letting people assume it, and allowing nothing to happen that will shake that assumption. This means that the people who finally appear on the programme should be people of whom you are known to approve, and you therefore immediately start writing to those you don't approve of, telling them in violent, obscene language to lie low. You believe that the more vicious and filthy the letters are, the more terrified the recipients will be. You start with Mrs Buller and her daughter, perhaps, and then the vicar, and so on. After a time, I imagine you started enjoying your feeling of power, of making people uneasy and afraid, so you wrote more letters than you needed to, though probably you were quite happy to keep people like Mr Billington and Mr Jimson off the programme if you could. Sometimes you had something to go on in these letters – village gossip, old local history and scandal – but sometimes you had nothing, I would guess. I wonder if you had any reason to suppose that Mr Jimson seduces little girls, for example? But you knew that the mere suspicion of anything of that sort is fatal to a schoolteacher. And you enjoy thinking up things of that nature.'

The frigid mask had not slipped a fraction, nor was a sound heard beyond her short intakes of breath.

'The letters stopped when the murder took place. Naturally, you were terrified that the two things might be connected. The last was to Mr Edgar – following a phone call from Miss Potts last Monday, I would guess, telling you what she saw at the amenities meeting. Now, Mrs Withens, I think if you will just confirm what I've said, and answer a few questions, we might come to an agreement.'

There was not a whisper of sound. Even the breathing was stilled.

'If you'll admit what you've done, there is a chance of hushing the whole thing up altogether, apart from informing my superiors.'

Stony, impenetrable silence.

'Then, Mrs Withens,' said Parrish, getting up, 'I shall have to ask you to come along with me to the station.'

Not a muscle twitched.

'I have a constable in the car. I presume you would not like to be dragged out of your own house. It is Saturday morning. There are plenty of people around outside to watch it happening.'

In a series of drugged movements, as if she were in the last hours of a dance marathon, Mrs Withens rose from her chair. Her face was set in a parody of a tragic mask, and she forced her limbs forward as if in some kind of indescribable internal pain.

'You might need a coat, ma'am,' said Parrish as they came to the hall. She took her fawn spring coat from the cupboard, and put on her round flat hat with the unidentifiable flowers and the little wisp of veil. With every minute her movements became slower and heavier. Parrish stood by the front door, watching her.

'Then perhaps we'd better be off, ma'am. Unless of course you would like to change your mind.'

She stood still, her expression and bearing showing her to be on the verge of collapse. Her voice, when it came, was a low, hollow croak, less like Clara Butt than Boris Christoff singing against doctor's orders.

'Very well,' said Deborah Withens.

It was not the most explicit of confessions, but President Nixon had been allowed to get away with less.

'Shall we go back to the drawing-room?' Parrish said. Deborah Withens, recovering, stalked before him, and sat down, her coat still on, her face set in an expression of vicious foreboding. She looked like the bride's mother waiting to be driven to church.

'Now, Mrs Withens,' said Parrish. 'I'll make a bargain with you. As far as the police are concerned, we can consider the matter closed if you will answer a couple of questions. Of course we may have to have a word with your husband – '

'Ernest!' said Mrs Withens, her voice throbbing with tragic emotion.

' – because we don't want a repetition. Beyond that we'll keep the whole thing secret. But I must know a few things first.'

Mrs Withens turned her head a fraction, as a signal of assent.

'You sent one of these letters to the Mailers, did you not?'

A nod, almost infinitesimal.

'Was it to Mrs or Mr Mailer?'

'Mister.' The hollow tone had returned.

'What did it say?'

There was a pause.

'Do you want the exact words?' croaked Mrs Withens.

'If you can recall them.'

' "Your cold bitch of a wife," ' intoned Mrs Withens, in a voice scarcely more than a whisper, ' "has been selling information to Cullings and Dawson. Ask her how much Jack Cullings gave her for the details of your tender on the new secondary school." '

It was not quite what Parrish had expected.

'I see,' he said at last. 'Was this just a shot in the dark?'

There was a barely perceptible negative.

'How did you know?'

A strange expression came into Mrs Withens's face, as if she were congratulating herself on her detective work.

'Mailer's firm puts in for most of the council contracts. The tendering is secret. Cullings and Dawson have been putting in bids just below theirs for more than a year. Ernest puts all the council business before me. Naturally. I could see there was a regular leak of information.'

'Why Mrs Mailer?'

'I followed her into Griffin's in Barstowe a week or so ago. She went to the tearooms. I thought there must be something. It's not fashionable enough for *her*. Jack Cullings was there, and she went past his table. They pretended it was an accidental meeting, but they didn't deceive *me*. They just shook hands, but she passed something to him — a bit of paper. It was obvious what it was.'

'I see,' said Parrish. 'Does it worry you, Mrs Withens, that your letter probably killed Mrs Mailer?'

There was no need to ask. The face had set itself into its accustomed mask of self-approval. The shoulders had straightened to their usual determined angularity, as if prepared to fight single-handed against the moral shortcomings of the rest of the world. Mrs Withens had already justified herself to herself, and was preparing a face to meet the faces that she met.

CHAPTER XIV

EN FAMILLE

The atmosphere in the police car was not a happy one as Inspector Parrish drove Stephen Feather out to the Mailers'. Stephen felt that he had been had : seven solid hours of interrogating Jimson, when his boss had known all the time he had had nothing to do with it, or was as near certain as makes no difference. He was not placated by being told that the motive had been the desire to give him experience of top-level interrogation, and that this had been a heaven-sent and unique opportunity. One reason for not being placated was a nagging suspicion that he had bungled over the bank-account business, and that with a tricky customer like Timothy Jimson this was unlikely to be the last they heard of it. Stephen looked broodily out into the torpid bustle of Twytching on Saturday morning. The Radio Broadwich van was parked outside the Lamb, and the technicians were loading in the last wisps of equipment. Hank was exchanging addresses with all and sundry, in the open-handed manner of one who knows he is quite safe from a visit. Harold was supervising, and Ted Livermore was standing sheepishly in the shadows. He had his arm in a sling and a black eye. Twytching's week of glory and Ted's of bliss had ended simultaneously.

Arnold Mailer and Cressida looked as if they had been about to go shopping in town. But they were friendly, dumped their bags down in the kitchen, and Mailer gestured Parrish up the stairs towards his little study. Parrish shook his head.

'I think I'd like to speak to both of you together,' he said.

. They went into the cool, airless lounge, with its white leather suite, and its chrome, and its air of nondescript taste. As soon as he had asked to talk with them both, Parrish had sensed a jittery element enter the atmosphere, and Arnold Mailer began talking too loudly. Parrish thought it was as well to get it over with as soon as possible. When they had sat down on their cold, expandable, adjustable, gently turning and rocking chairs, Parrish took out his notes and his bits and pieces of evidence, and began his unenviable task.

'Cressida,' he said. 'I have an exercise book here. One of your English ones from Barstowe Grammar School.'

'Oh yes,' said Cressida, flashing him a child-like smile.

'I saw you'd taken them. I wondered what you wanted them for.'

'Now, do you remember writing an essay in this book, just after Easter? It was about Easter, in fact. And what you did with your mother – the walks you took, and so on.'

The child's eyes started swimming with tears. 'Yes, I remember it,' she said.

'When exactly did you write that piece, Cressida?' said Parrish, very gently.

'Isn't it dated?' said Cressida vaguely. 'I think it was the first subject Mr Jimson gave us this term.'

'It is dated, yes,' said Parrish. 'But there's something odd about this essay. Do you see?' He handed the book across to her. 'The page that it's written on is a little bit larger than the page on either side of it – it protrudes over their edges very slightly.'

Cressida nodded, and seemed about to speak.

'And if you look in the middle of the book,' said Parrish, hurrying forward to get the girl out of it, 'where it's stapled together, you'll see that the staple holes on this page don't quite correspond with the others – new ones have had to be made, to fit this page in. So it looks as if you've taken a page from another exercise book and put it in here. See, if you follow the page through, back to the first half of the exercise book, it looks as if you've had to rewrite parts of two of your earlier essays. The ink is slightly different in shade. And you've had to put in Mr Jimson's marks as well, in both places.'

It was out. There was complete silence in the room, and one could almost see in Cressida Mailer's young face the working of her brain. Arnold Mailer seemed about to speak, but Parrish stopped him.

'May I put a case to you, Cressida? I think that one day over Easter or after you were playing with the Jimson children, and you were getting cards and games and things out of their sideboard, and you found a letter at the bottom of all the muddle there – a very funny-looking letter, which made you read it. It said . . . it accused Mr Jimson of . . . of some rather unpleasant things. Perhaps you didn't understand. Perhaps you asked someone about them. I don't know. But I think you remembered this after your mummy died. And I think you made sure that whenever anyone saw you after that, you were writing, or had a pen in your hand. Eventually someone was going to think "that little girl's always writing. I wonder if she saw anything that might provide a clue!" Even a dumb policeman might think of that. And they were going to be led straight off on to a false scent, probably leading them towards Mr Jimson, which is exactly what happened for a bit. That exercise book was what they call a put-up job, wasn't it, Cressida? Now, why would you want to send us off on a false scent?'

'To protect me, Inspector,' said Arnold Mailer. He rose sharply from his chair, with a sort of resignation about the gesture, as if he considered himself already under arrest, and was relieved, and wanted to be going.

'No!' said Cressida.

'That's what I thought, sir,' said Parrish. As they both stood face to face he noticed again what a big man Arnold Mailer was. As a rule his self-effacing courtesy, and his gentleness, rather hid that. Sometimes he almost seemed not to be there. But his sudden gesture drew all eyes to himself, and even Feather noticed it, and the bigness of his hands.

'She did it to protect me, Inspector,' he said. 'I didn't know about it until after the exercise books were taken away, or I would have made her tear it out. Can we get this over as quickly as possible, Inspector? I suppose you know by now what happened?'

'I know that you did in fact receive an anonymous letter,' said Parrish. 'It was silly to deny it. I also have a very fair idea of what it contained.'

Arnold Mailer drew his hand across his forehead. 'Then

you'll know it was a pretty nasty shock. Last Saturday it was. Seems much longer. At first I thought it must be some nasty-minded crank. I decided to ignore it. I wish to hell I had. But you go on thinking about these things, that's the devil of it. They sort of fester. This one did, anyway. It tied in with so much – the loss of these contracts we'd been putting in for in this area, things that we'd normally be able to bank on, or at least get our share of. Not matters of life and death to a big firm like ours, but useful. And then, I'd been worried recently because Alison had been buying things which she didn't seem to expect me to pay for. I thought she was running up bills, and I was afraid they were going to all descend on me at once. But they never came. I'd decided she must have been saving money out of her allowance, and yet . . . well, it didn't seem likely. So it all hung together, and I thought and thought about it all weekend.'

'And you set a trap?' asked Parrish.

'Yes. Does that sound dreadful? I couldn't think of any other way. It was the simple, old-fashioned sort. I left my briefcase in the study, and stuck a hair over the envelope containing the details of our tender for a new fire-station in Croxham. That was Monday. Then I went to the amenities meeting.'

'And when you got back the hair was unstuck.'

'Oh yes, it was unstuck.' Mailer drew his hands through his hair and looked very tired. Parrish wondered how many hours' sleep he had had since Monday. But he shook the weariness out of himself, and continued: 'I don't know if you know, Inspector, but Alison was my secretary before we married. She knew all about the business, what to look for, where it would be, who would be interested in buying the information.' His voice was bitter. 'I loved her all our married life, and yet I don't suppose she thought twice about what she was doing.'

There was nothing anyone could say to that. If there was ever anybody whose thoughts were all for one person, it was Alison Mailer.

'But you must realize,' resumed Mailer, 'that it was just done for the money – not to spite me, or anything. I have no money myself in Allington's – that's my firm. She knew we would suffer no financial harm, at least not in the short term. She never could think further than that. She just wanted pocket-money for herself. It's difficult to imagine – for me – still. I bought her everything she asked for, if it was humanly possible. We've never saved, always lived up to our income, because there's always been something she wanted. I suppose the more she had, the more she wanted, and so eventually she had to do this. I realize I didn't know her.'

'So what did you do?' asked Parrish gently.

'She was in the kitchen, making herself a nightcap. We started to – well, what can you say, except that we had a row? She hardly bothered to deny what she'd done: it almost seemed as though she – she despised me too much to bother. She started sneering – at what I earned, and so on. Said she expected me to have made the big time by now, got on, moved to London, expected us to have made friends with people who mattered. She didn't bother to wrap this up in fine words – it all came out, just like that. It was all so petty, so vulgar, and selfish. I hate to think of it.'

'But she touched a raw nerve?'

'What? Oh, I suppose so. Suddenly I saw red, some sort of pure rage came over me. She turned away – you know that graceful way she had – as if the matter was too trivial to concern her anymore. There was a cutlet bat on the table – '

'A what, sir?'

'One of those heavy things you bash meat with. To make the slices thinner. We'd had Wiener Schnitzel for dinner, and she'd been using it. I took it up and hit her with it twice. She fell on the kitchen table. And that's really all there was to it, Inspector. Would you let me say goodbye to Cressida, and then we'll – '

'It's not true!'

'Cressida!' Mailer's voice shot out with whiplash clarity, and he took both her wrists in his hands, and seemed to be squeezing them until Cressida gasped with pain. He looked into her eyes, hard, and then let her arms drop, and made sharply for the door, motioning Parrish to follow him. But Cressida was not to be silenced so easily.

'It's not true,' she repeated, sucking her red wrists, and looking at Parrish with a terrible intensity, passion burning in her eyes. The furious obstinacy of the expression suggested to Parrish something she must have got from her mother. 'Daddy's telling you this to cover up for me. He wants to shield me. It wasn't like that.'

Conscious that she had all eyes on her, and that she could not now be ignored, Cressida sat down again, and seemed to be reliving the scene.

'I'd been reading, and I heard them quarrelling. I came downstairs. Mother was standing on one side of the kitchen table, Daddy was walking around. She was saying horrible things, that woman, disgusting things in that calm, snaky voice of hers. The cutlet bat was on the dresser. I'd used it to make dinner. I made the dinner. I always made the dinner, and that woman pretended I just helped, as if I was playing. I took the bat. They hadn't seen me because they were starting to shout. It's very heavy. I swung it, and bashed the back of her head, like I had the meat.'

'This is nonsense, Inspector, utter nonsense,' shouted Arnold Mailer. 'Just sick fantasies.'

'She fell forward on to the table. It had a plastic cloth on. She was completely still. Daddy turned around, and he looked for a moment as if he couldn't believe it. Then he ran over and took the bat, and hit her with it again, with the side. "Now no one can say you killed her," he said. He did it for me, but she was dead already. I know it.'

No one said anything, for there was nothing to say. Arnold Mailer was looking desperate, and finally he turned to

Parrish. 'This is the most horrible nonsense, Inspector. You know a child would never do a thing like that. She's been completely upset by this whole business. She doesn't know what she's saying.'

'I think your father's right, Cressida,' said Parrish slowly. 'Why would a little girl like you do a thing like that to her mother?'

'I'm not a little girl. I'm twelve, and quite big for my age. I did it because I hated her.'

'Now that's nonsense, Cressida –'

'It's not nonsense.' Suddenly the whole body of the child seemed to be shaken by the passion in the eyes, and a furious energy seized her. Her hands clasped and unclasped themselves, as she tried to find words. 'Nobody's ever hated anyone as I hated her. She was cold and selfish and – disgusting!' The body shook with frustration that she could bring out no better word than that. 'She never cared a bit for me, or for Daddy. Only for herself. She thought of herself all day. She never even spoke to me if there was no one around, except to sneer – because I liked reading and writing, because I loved Daddy, anything she could think of. She just used me to do things, to do the cooking and all that kind of thing. She pretended to Daddy I'd just helped. *Helped*! As if I were a baby! She hated Daddy and me. She hated seeing us together. She was saying filthy things about us when I killed her – as if there was something wrong in loving each other. I'd kill her again. I wish I could. The main thing is that she's dead. I don't care about anything else, so long as she's dead.'

The little chin went up, and the eyes still blazed.

'What did you do after that?' asked Parrish.

'Well, we sat around, and discussed what to do with her.' There was something monstrous about this new life and vitality in the child. She talked as if what she was remembering was the cosiness of the discussion, the conspiring together with her father – and it was how to get rid of her mother. 'Daddy was upset at first, so I had to take the decisions. I decided we should wait until later, when we could be sure everyone was asleep, then put her somewhere where she wouldn't be found till next day. Obviously we couldn't just leave her there. Luckily the plastic table-cloth was the only thing with blood on, and there wasn't too much. We wrapped her in it, and Daddy drove as near as he could to the bluebell woods, and then dumped her.'

Dumped her. There was relish in the voice. The egotism of this terrible, imaginative child came from her mother. The only thing that mattered to her was that she had felt rejected, and had had her revenge. It was an equation with all the brutal simplicity of childhood. No other calculations entered into it, just transgression and retribution.

'Then we tied stones to the table-cloth, wrapped it round the cutlet bat, and sank it in Wilcher's bog. Daddy thought of that. He said it was forty foot deep, and the things would never be found. Then we came home and Daddy slept a bit. I had to think about things, and I made sure he got up next morning and went to London as usual. After that he became quite good at lying. Because he was doing it for me, you see. It would have been different if he had been doing it for himself. We lied to you all the time, of course. We had to. He was lying just now. Because I killed her. She was dead when she hit the table. I'd thought of doing it for ages. Absolute ages.'

She looked straight at Parrish, the expression on her face one of obstinate self-congratulation. She seemed to be almost challenging him to deny what she said. Looking at her, at the strength and energy and passion, Parrish could not deny it. This, he felt sure, was the truth. But with a heavy heart he turned and arrested Arnold Mailer.

CHAPTER XV

AFTERWARDS

Naturally the murder was the main topic of conversation in the saloon bar of the Lamb that Sunday lunch-time. Murder was one of those subjects that drew everyone together, like inflation, or Enoch Powell.

'I'd never have thought it,' said Dr McGregor, sipping his whisky, 'not in a thousand years. Not at all the type.'

'Not writing those letters,' said Mrs Leaze from her table. 'To think of a quiet type like 'im writing filth like that.'

'Still waters run deep,' said Mrs Brewer sagely, as if she had just thought of it.

'He didn't write the letters,' said Jack Edgar. 'He's only accused of the murder, not writing the letters.'

'Well if 'e didn't, 'oo did?' said Mrs Leaze with finality. Everyone saw the force of her argument.

'Course he did,' said Val Rice. 'I think he must have fancied me, you know. I expect he needed the warmer type.'

'She was *cold*,' said Mrs Leaze.

'Terribly cold,' agreed everyone.

'I expect she'd been unfaithful,' said Jack Edgar. 'Eh, Tom?'

'Yers,' said Tom Billington, looking furious.

'Parrish was at the Withenses' on Saturday morning,' said Mrs Brewer. 'What price she and Ernest had been having it off?'

There was a general guffaw.

'There's one mercy,' said Mrs Buller. 'It's no reflection on the town. Because they weren't locals, were they? He was a nice chap, but he was never one of us. Nor was she.'

They nodded sagely over their glasses, conscious of being of the elect.

Sunday was a day of rest and recuperation for Timothy Jimson, and he screamed for peace at every sign of noise or activity from his family. This was his way of reasserting himself after the damaging lack of respect shown him by Sergeant Feather. But by Sunday he had regrouped his forces, had marshalled a high degree of self-righteousness to come to the aid of his self-importance, and had grafted on to these an entirely new element, namely that hitherto much despised thing, a social conscience. His experiences with the police were to be the start of a new campaign, one to protect the ordinary citizen, inform the general public of the abuse of power taking place under their noses, and alert the media in order to bring the maximum of publicity to bear. He was very insistent on these last points : alert the media; the maximum of publicity.

After Jean and the children had finished the big wash-up following Sunday lunch, she found Timothy sitting in his armchair, his fingers intertwined over his little stomach, planning plans.

'It seems to me we ought to start with *The Times,*' he said. 'Always a good place to start, provided you take the right tone. I'd aim at a simple, sober statement of fact, nothing shrill : the inquisition, the forced overnight stay to soften me up, the *outrageous* use of my bank account.' He realized he was becoming shrill, and lowered his voice. 'Then perhaps we could use the radio and TV. Yes, definitely. Appeal for other people's experiences to compile a dossier from. What could we call it : the black book?'

'The idea's been used,' said Jean.

'Yes, well – that's a detail. Obviously we can orchestrate the campaign from here. Get in the letters, file them, make them public in bursts, every few months, to keep the topic on the boil. Show the public they have certain rights vis-à-vis the police.'

'Aren't there other bodies?' said Jean. 'The Civil Liberties people, for example?'

'Really, Jean,' said Timothy. 'They hardly helped much in my case, did they? They've been going for *decades,* but the same bullying and prying still goes on. Obviously we need a completely new body, one that concentrates on the one thing, being a watchdog on the police. There'll be acres of correspondence, of course. I do so wish you were a typist, Jean. It would mean I didn't have to do *all* the work myself.'

'Oh, I shan't be here,' said Jean. 'I'm leaving you.'

Timothy was much too taken up with his plans to understand.

'Jean, *really*! What a time to go away. It's no time at all since you went to your mother's last. Though, there again, it might give me a bit of peace from the children . . .'

'That's right,' said Jean. 'Permanent peace. I shall be leaving for good.'

Timothy looked at her disbelievingly. 'This isn't the time for a joke, Jean. You know I'm still emotionally upset by this whole business. Shattered, in fact. I'm afraid I'm not finding it funny.'

Jean knew Timothy hated her using literary clichés, but she couldn't find any other way of saying it.

'I . . . am . . . leaving . . you . . . for . . . good.'

'But that's nonsense,' said Timothy. 'You've never given the slightest hint of this before. We've always been perfectly happy. What possible reason could you have?'

'I haven't been happy. I find you selfish, pompous and conceited. If you've been happy it's because your big need is for someone you think you can despise and bully. Other than that, you won't notice if we're not here. Those are the reasons. I shall be leaving by tomorrow night.'

And she left the room.

Timothy still didn't believe it. Of course she must have been upset by this silly business. Surely she couldn't have believed that ridiculous letter? She'd get over it, anyway.

Women are basically silly creatures, Timothy thought, but eventually they get over whatever was bothering them. Meanwhile he wasn't going to let it spoil his afternoon. Radio Broadwich were putting out *This Is Twytching* at three, and that was something to look forward to. He would just sit down and think about that.

'You're still unhappy about the case, aren't you?' said Betty Underwood as they sat in the smoky atmosphere of the police station with the afternoon sun streaming in the windows.

'Of course I'm unhappy about it,' said Parrish. 'Do you think I like arresting the wrong man?'

'You can't be sure about that,' said Feather.

'Not one hundred per cent sure, anymore than you could be that Charlie Crippen murdered his wife,' said Parrish. 'But you saw the little girl yesterday, Stephen. I expect you thought exactly what I thought.'

Stephen nodded.

'It's a really hideous thing, if so,' said Sergeant Underwood.

'Oh it's hideous, all right. So hideous that no jury would believe it if they had an alternative. But it's a much better story than her father's. I never did believe in these quiet complacent husbands who suddenly turn round and kill their wives – not unless there's sex involved. "Some sort of pure rage came over me," Arnold Mailer said. That was something he'd read, not something he'd experienced. Left alone the thing would have simmered for a week or two, Mailer would have had a new lock put on his briefcase, and that would have been the end of it.'

'Do you think he was as blind to the sort of woman she was as he says?' asked Stephen.

'Oh yes, I think so. Probably that was one of the things that drove the daughter to desperation. Of course he loves her too, worships her, obviously. And when he saw what she'd done, he leapt straight in and made sure he was implicated to the hilt. But that sort gets adept at sentiment-alizing. Things have to be as they ought to be : mothers and daughters *must* love one another – it's nature. But, in fact, to Alison Mailer her daughter was a bore and a bind.'

'Such a clever little girl too,' said Betty.

'Clever? Clever as a waggon-load of monkeys. Did you see those tears in the eyes when we first mentioned those fictitious Easter walks with her mother, Stephen? But of course Alison didn't necessarily like clever people, far from it. And in Cressida, well, there you have another little monster of egotism. The two egotisms clashed. She felt the hatred and contempt flowing from her mother, and she nursed up this intense, fierce, passionate hatred. It's a terrible thought, but we all say that children are growing up earlier these days, and that means they're beginning to get all sorts of adult emotions early, not just the sexual ones. They're exposed to the adult world all the time, in one way or another. We think that someone who does this sort of thing has to be a Glasgow tough, or someone like that, but kids all over are subject to the same sort of pressures. They drove this one inside herself, bottling up all sorts of hatreds and jealousies and hopes of revenge.'

'I can't say I like the thought of sending her to relatives,' said Sergeant Underwood. 'Couldn't you make it stick?'

'In the normal course of events I could,' said Parrish. 'But with the father standing up there and saying he did it, with a perfectly good motive, and all the evidence at least as good for him as for her – well, no jury on earth, or no magistrate, would do anything about the girl. As it is, the best we can do is get Mailer on a manslaughter charge – reduce the sentence a bit. He sure as hell was an accessory, and there's just a chance she wasn't dead when he hit her. As justice it's pretty rough and ready, but sometimes in this job "the best we can do" is what we have to do. You'll learn that, I'm afraid, both of you.'

'It doesn't seem fair,' said Betty, 'him getting the full works and that monster Deborah Withens going back to queening it over the town as if nothing had happened.'

'It wasn't fair,' said Parrish. 'Necessary, but not fair. I had to make the bargain or the thing would have dragged on till kingdom come. Still, I don't think I'll ever be able to look Ernest in the eye again.'

'But you gave him his chance,' said Stephen. 'You told her you'd tell him about the letters, you gave him a hold over her. It's up to him to use it – assert himself.'

'That's like those bloody pirates who shove people off in an open boat with a crust of bread and a glass of water and say, "Isn't it nice of us not making you walk the plank? We've given you a chance." The only way he'll be rescued from that woman is by death. And I'd bet it won't be hers. Would you take on a bet who'll be cooking the breakfast tomorrow morning?'

But Stephen wouldn't take him on.

'So now we go back to being the same sleepy, nasty little town – damn!'

'What?'

'The programme's started. We've missed five minutes of it.'

'Lucky old us,' said Betty Underwood, turning on the radio.

For the next fifty minutes all was silence: they sat through an impressionistic rendering of a typical British pub at closing-time; they sat through a typical British fish and chip shop on a Friday night; they sat through swelling oceans of cliché from Hank on the concern of the British for their senior citizens. They sat through 'Because', sung by Mario Lanza, through the Dance of the Little Swans, through Bing Crosby singing 'If I Can Help Somebody', and through 'An English Country Garden'.

'I hate to think it,' said Parrish at the end, 'but I'm awfully afraid Timothy Jimson has missed the bus. It doesn't seem to be his weekend.'

'That, Ernest,' said Deborah Withens settling herself back

in her chair, 'that was exactly the sort of programme I have been wanting. Exactly what I've been working for. I think we can be proud, proud and happy. We've put our best foot forward, and presented the world with a model little community. Most gratifying!'

She tapped her spoon on her saucer.

'Another cup of tea, I think, Ernest.'